Of Blood

Lee Fenton opened her eyes with a sense of coming back from a very long way off.

She sat up frowning. A dream—that was what it was. She had had a perfect beast of a dream, and some of the nightmare feeling was still hanging around.

She couldn't remember the dream, but it must have been a particularly bad one for her to feel like this. She threw the sheet right off her, swung her legs over the edge of the bed, and stayed there staring, with a hand on either side of her, pressing down hard upon the mattress and the old linen sheet which covered it.

The hem of her pale pink nightgown was stained deep with blood...

THE BLIND SIDE

Also by Patricia Wentworth

BEGGAR'S CHOICE
THE CASE IS CLOSED
THE CLOCK STRIKES TWELVE
DEAD OR ALIVE
THE FINGERPRINT
GREY MASK
THE LISTENING EYE
LONESOME ROAD
PILGRIM'S REST
MR. ZERO
NOTHING VENTURE
OUTRAGEOUS FORTUNE
RUN!
THE WATERSPLASH
WICKED UNCLE

Published by
WARNER BOOKS

PATRICIA WENTWORTH

THE BLIND SIDE

WARNER BOOKS

A Time Warner Company

WARNER BOOKS EDITION

Copyright © 1939 by J. B. Lippincott Company
All rights reserved.

This Warner Books Edition is published by arrangement with Harper & Row Publishers, Inc., 10 East 53rd Street, New York, N.Y. 10022

Cover design by Anne Twomey
Cover illustration by Bob Scott

Warner Books, Inc.
1271 Avenue of the Americas
New York, N.Y. 10020

W A Time Warner Company

Printed in the United States of America

First Warner Books Printing: June, 1991

10 9 8 7 6 5 4 3

CHAPTER

I

CRADDOCK HOUSE STANDS at the end of one of those streets which run between the Kings Road and the Embankment. From the third and fourth floor windows you can see the trees which fringe the river, and the river beyond the trees. David Craddock built it with the money he made in railways just over ninety years ago. His son John Peter and his daughters Mary and Elinor were young and gay there. They danced in the big drawing-room, supped under glittering chandeliers in the enormous dining-room, and slept in those rooms whose windows looked to the river. Mary married her cousin Andrew Craddock and went away with him to Birmingham, and in due course she had three daughters. The others married too. John Peter's wife brought a good deal more money into the family. Elinor ran away with an impecunious young artist called John Lee, and was cut off without a shilling. Their daughter Ann made an equally penniless match with one James Fenton, a schoolmaster, and both, dying young, left their daughter Lee to fight for a place in the world without any inheritance except a gay heart. John Peter had a son and daughter by his plain, rich wife—the son John David, and the daughter another Mary. John, marrying Miss Marian Ross, became the father of Ross Craddock, and Mary, marrying James Renshaw, produced also an only son, Peter Craddock Renshaw.

It was Ross Craddock's father who had turned Craddock House into flats. His wife Marian said that Chelsea was damp, and they moved away to Highgate. The big rooms cut up well, a lift was installed, and the flats brought in an excellent return for the money John David had spent on them. He retained the middle flat on the third floor for his own use, and installed his Aunt Mary's daughters, Lucy and Mary Craddock, in the flats on either side. People laughed a good deal, his brother-in-law James Renshaw going so far as to speak about John's harem. But John David had never cared in the least what anybody said about anything. Lucy and Mary were his first cousins, and he felt responsible for them. They had neither looks, cash, nor common sense. They were alone in the world, and Mary was in poor health. He put them into separate flats because, though sincerely attached to one another, they could not help quarrelling. He considered it an admirable arrangement and as fixed as any natural ordinance. It never occurred to him to mind the cackle of fools or to dream that his son Ross would turn poor Lucy adrift as soon as the breath was out of Mary's body.

Nobody could have dreamed it, least of all Miss Lucy Craddock herself. She had read the wicked, unbelievable letter fifty times and still she couldn't believe it, because they had lived here for thirty years, she in No. 7 and Mary in No. 9, and John David had meant them to live here always. And now Mary was dead and Ross had written this dreadful letter. She read it at breakfast, and ran incredulously to knock at the door of Ross Craddock's flat. Ross couldn't possibly mean what he had written—he couldn't. But there was no answer to her knocking on the door of No. 8, and no answer when she rang the bell.

She ran across the landing to No. 9. Peter Renshaw would tell her that it was all nonsense. Ross couldn't possibly turn her out. But she could get no answer there either, and then remembered that Peter was away for the night, gone down to stay with a friend in the country. Of course it was very tiresome for him being poor Mary's executor and having all those papers to sort through, but she did wish he wasn't away just now. Perhaps he would be back before she had to start on her journey. Perhaps she ought not to start—not if Ross really meant what he said. But perhaps he didn't mean it—perhaps there was some mistake—perhaps there wasn't. Oh, dear, dear, dear—how could she possibly go away if she was going to be turned out of her flat? But she had promised dear Mary. She had promised to go away as soon as possible after the funeral. She had promised faithfully. Oh dear, dear, dear!

She went back to her own flat and packed her little cane trunk, and then went trotting over to No. 8 in case Ross had returned, and to No. 9 to see if Peter had come back. She kept on doing this for hours. Sometimes she packed her things, and sometimes she unpacked them. At intervals she read the cruel letter again, and about once in every half hour she rang the bells of No. 8 and 9.

"Like a cat on hot bricks!" Rush, the porter, told his bedridden wife in the basement. "What's she want to go away for?"

"Everyone wants to get away some time," said Mrs. Rush mildly. She sat up against four pillows and knitted baby socks for her daughter Ellen's youngest, who was expecting in a month's time. She was pale, and plump, and clean, with very little thin white hair screwed up into a pigtail, and a white flannelette nightgown trimmed with tatting.

"I don't," said Rush, "and no more do you. A lot of blasted nonsense I call it!"

Mrs. Rush opened her mouth to speak and shut it again. She hadn't been out of her basement room for fifteen years, but that wasn't to say she wouldn't have liked to go. Men were all the same—if they didn't fancy a thing themselves, then no one else wasn't to fancy it neither. She began to turn the heel of the little woolly sock.

Ross Craddock came home just before three o'clock in the afternoon. He took himself up in the lift, and as soon as Miss Lucy heard the clang of the gate she opened her front door a crack and looked out. It was really Ross at last. Her heart bumped against her side and her breath caught in her throat. He looked as he always did, so very handsome and so masterful. It was ridiculous to feel afraid of someone she had seen christened, but there was something about Ross that made you feel as if you didn't matter at all.

She stood behind the door and gathered up her courage, a little roundabout woman with a straight grey bob and a full pale face. She wore a dyed black dress which had been navy blue and her best all the summer, and low-heeled strap shoes over thick grey stockings. When she heard Ross Craddock put his key into the lock she popped out of her door and ran after him. If he had seen her, she would not have caught him up. But Miss Lucy was not without cunning. She timed her trembling rush so that it took her through the half open door and into the little hall beyond.

Ross Craddock, removing his key, was aware that he had been caught. He said suavely, "You want to see me, do you?" and opened the sitting-room door.

Miss Lucy walked in and stood there trembling with his letter in her hand. She saw him come in after her, remove his hat, and sit down at the writing-table half turned away. When she said "*Yes*" in a loud, angry voice, he swung his chair round a little and surveyed her with a faint smile upon his face.

Miss Lucy came a step nearer. She pushed the letter towards him as if it could speak for her. It was a hot August day and her skin was beaded with moisture. She said, her voice fallen to a whisper,

"You didn't mean it—you didn't."

"And what makes you think that, Lucy?"

He was smiling more broadly now. Such a good-looking man, so tall, and strong, and handsome. It didn't seem possible that he could really mean to be so unkind. She said,

"But, Ross—"

"A month's notice," said Ross Craddock exactly as if she had been a kitchenmaid.

Miss Lucy stopped trembling. She was too angry to tremble now.

"Your father put us here—he gave us the flats—he said he would never turn us out!"

"It isn't my father who is turning you out, Lucy."

Miss Lucy looked at him. There was a big photograph of Mavis on the table at his elbow. Mavis was her own niece—Mavis Grey. It was a new photograph, one that she had never seen before, and she was ashamed to see it now. It looked like one of those shameless pictures sent in for beauty competitions, only instead of being an enlarged snapshot as most of them were, it was beautifully posed, beautifully taken—Mavis in what she supposed was some sort of fancy dress—tights, and a sort of feather frill, and a bodice cut so low that it wasn't really a bodice at all. A dull, ugly red came into her face.

Ross Craddock laughed.

"Good photograph, isn't it?" he said.

"Did Mavis give it to you?"

"Had it taken for me, Lucy."

"It's a scandalous picture!" said Lucy Craddock. "She's my niece—she's my own niece. And she's your cousin too, because my father and mother were cousins. And you ought to leave her alone—you know you ought. Why, what would anyone think who saw that picture?"

"That Mavis has a very good figure," said Ross Craddock. He fixed those dark eyes of his upon the photograph, and Miss Lucy's colour deepened.

"I asked you to leave her alone! I begged and prayed you to before Mary got so ill."

He said, "Exactly," and turned his eyes upon the letter, which she still held clasped in her hand.

"And that's why you're turning me out?"

"My dear Lucy—what penetration!"

She went back a step. Her colour faded.

"How *wicked!*" she said.

Ross Craddock got up. He took her lightly by the arm and led her to the door.

"Old maid cousins should be seen and not heard," he said, and put her out.

CHAPTER

II

S HE WAS STILL there on the landing when Peter Renshaw
came running up the stairs about five minutes later. He
was a tall young man—all the Craddock men ran to
height—but he had none of his cousin's claim to good
looks. Rather jutting brows, rather prominent cheek bones,
rather wide-set eyes, a skin tanned by the Indian sun, a
small nondescript moustache, hair that had once been very
fair and had never quite made up its mind to go brown—that
was Peter Renshaw. He was thirty years of age, held His
Majesty's commission in the Westshire Regiment, and was
at present on leave from India.

He stopped on the top step and contemplated his Cousin
Lucy with some astonishment. She had her back to him and
her face to Ross Craddock's front door, and she was shaking
her fist at it, absolutely and literally shaking her fist. Peter
couldn't recall having ever seen anyone actually shake a fist
before. A slight whistle escaped him. Lucy Craddock turned
round and showed him a strangely unfamiliar face, tear-
stained, heavily flushed, and quite distorted by anger.

"Hullo, Lucinda—what's up?"

At the sound of his voice she burst out crying. She clung
to his arm.

"He's wicked!" she said, and choked, and sobbed it out
again.

Peter unlocked the door of No. 9 and got her inside. If Lucy must have hysterics, let her have them in decent privacy. He put her on the couch which had been her sister's, pulled up a chair, and said briskly,

"What's Ross been doing now?"

She was in such a state of agitation that it took him some time to arrive at the facts. He had to disentangle the Mavis motif from the eviction motif, and in the end he wasn't quite sure which was upsetting poor Lucinda most. Mavis was none of his business, and he certainly wasn't going to have a row with Ross about her, but the eviction was a different matter. He was quite prepared to fight if there was the faintest chance of success. He patted Lucy's heaving shoulder and said,

"All right. Now take a breather. No, you've cried enough. Here's my handkerchief. Blow the nose, brace the back, and listen to your Uncle Peter."

Miss Lucy sniffed against the cold clean linen, dabbed her eyes with a shaking hand, and gazed at him with touching confidence. Peter wouldn't let her be turned out. Peter would speak to Ross.

"Now," said Peter, "what I want to know is just this. When Uncle John brought you and Mary here, did you have a lease or anything like that?"

"It's such a long time ago—I'm sure I never thought—"

"Think now," he said. "Think as hard as you can. Are you sure there wasn't a lease?"

"Oh, I don't know—oh, I'm sure there wasn't—but if there had been—Mary would have known—and she didn't always tell me things—of course she ought to have—but she didn't—"

Peter patted her again.

"Don't bother. If Mary had anything, I'll find it—it'll be somewhere in the welter. But think. Did Uncle John ever write to you about your coming here?"

"Oh, no—he was so kind—he came to see us. We were in very poor lodgings, you know—up in Birmingham—after Papa's death. He failed, you know—and then he died—and dear John came and fetched us away and gave us these flats—''

"He gave you the flats? What did he say?"

"Oh, I don't remember," said Lucy Craddock, and burst into a fresh flood of tears.

She really knew nothing. It took Peter another quarter of an hour to make quite sure of this. If there was any evidence as to John David's intention with regard to the flats, it would be somewhere in the muddle of papers Mary Craddock had left for him to sort. He very much feared that there wasn't going to be any evidence.

"And I don't know what to do," said Lucy, sobbing— "because I've got my tickets—and I'm all packed up—and the train goes at half past seven—but I can't go away now—can I?"

"Of course you can! Now look here, Lucinda, you've got to pull yourself together and carry on. You promised Mary you'd go away for a change, and you've got to keep your promise. Don't you see it's the very best thing you can do? If you go away you tie Ross's hands. He can't very well put your furniture out in the street, and anyhow I'll be here to see he doesn't. And you'll be giving me time to go through the rest of the papers. There may be something that'll give you a case. So you see, you couldn't do anything better than be out of the way for a bit. Now if you've still got anything to pack you'd better hop along and get on with it."

Lucy Craddock stopped crying. She had the relieved, exhausted feeling that comes after prolonged weeping. She wanted to go away and forget all about Ross Craddock. She said,

"Oh, do you think I could? But there's Mavis too. He's got a dreadful picture of her in there. She oughtn't to have let him have it. She ought not to go about with him. He's a very wicked man. I don't think I ought to go away and leave her."

"She is with her father's people, isn't she?"

"Yes—the Ernest Greys. She's very strict, but she hasn't any influence over Mavis. Besides, she doesn't know—" She broke off rather short and looked frightened.

"What doesn't she know?"

Lucy Craddock shook her head in a distracted manner.

"What is there to know?" said Peter.

Lucy shook her head again. Then she burst out,

"He can't marry her—he doesn't want to marry her—and he ought to leave her alone. She's my niece and his own cousin, and it's not *right!* And Mrs. Grey has no influence—Mavis doesn't listen to her."

"Does she listen to you, Lucinda?" said Peter.

"Oh, no, she doesn't. I don't know what girls are coming to. She doesn't listen to anyone."

"Then what's the use of your staying?"

Lucy Craddock jumped up.

"Oh!" she said, "I wish Ross was *dead!*" She ran out of the room and out of the flat, as if the sound of her own words frightened her.

CHAPTER
III

"OH, DEAR!", said Lucy Craddock.
She was all ready to start, her umbrella on her left wrist and the handle of her bag slipped over the umbrella handle in the special twist which she hoped would make it very difficult for a thief to snatch the bag whilst she was counting her luggage or tipping a porter. In her left hand she had the taxi fare all ready, and in her right she carried the little suitcase which contained everything she would need until she reached Marseilles.

And now there was the telephone bell ringing, and she would have to put everything down and keep the taxi waiting and—Her pale eyes looked distressfully out of her round pale face.

"Oh *dear!*" she said.

She took up the receiver, and heard Lee Fenton say,

"Is that you, Cousin Lucy?"

But it couldn't be Lee, because Lee must be on her way to South America by now. Quite against everyone's advice, but then young people never took advice.

She said in a small distracted voice, "Oh dear—who are you? I can't stay—I'm just starting."

Lee Fenton, in the station call-box, giggled and frowned. No need to ask if it was Cousin Lucy at the other end of the line. And what a fuss she was in. Anyhow thank goodness she hadn't started. She said firmly,

"Cousin Lucy, it's Lee. Please don't start till I've told you what I want."

Miss Lucy Craddock looked anxiously over her shoulder. The telephone was in the hall of the flat, a wall fixture, and if the kitchen door was open behind her she ought to be able to see the kitchen clock, and then she would know how much time she had to spare. But of course it wasn't open. She had shut all the doors herself, the kitchen door and the bathroom door behind her, and the bedroom door and the sitting-room door on her left. Only the front door stood open, just as Rush had left it when he carried down her trunk, and her hat-box, and the big suitcase which had poor Mary's initials on it but she hoped that wouldn't matter because there was an extra large label with her own name in full—Lucy Craddock.

She said in an agitated voice, "But, my dear—where are you? And I'm just starting—I really am."

"Darling, you always start half an hour too soon—you know you do. I'll be as quick as lightning, but you must listen. Are you listening?"

"Yes—yes—But haven't you sailed? I thought you were at sea—"

"Well, thank goodness I'm not. Darling, it was a wash-out."

"A wash-out?"

"Absolutely. And I shall put it across Madeleine Deshenka next time I see her—only I don't suppose I shall now, because from the way she talked you'd have thought she knew these Merville people in their cradles, and I only found out by accident two days before we were due to start that she'd picked them up in the Casino at Monte Carlo a couple of months ago, and all she really knew about them was that they'd made a packet."

Miss Lucy gave a horrified gasp.

"Oh, my dear—how dreadful! I always said—"

Lee made a face at her end of the line.

"Darling, I know you did. But this isn't the moment to trample—it really isn't."

"Oh, Lee, you can't go with people like that—not to South America—you really can't!"

"I'm not going. Anyhow it wasn't *them* any longer—it was *him*. They had a row—darling, I can't begin to tell you what a really first-class row it was—and then she walked out and took the little girl with her. And he seemed to think I was going to stay and just sail away with him into the blue, so I walked out too, and here I am."

"Where?"

"Victoria Station. Don't get rattled, darling—nothing has happened, and nothing is going to happen. But listen. Can I have the key of Cousin Mary's flat and stay there for a bit while I look round for something to bring in the shekels, because this has just about cleaned me out and it won't run to digs."

Miss Lucy felt, and sounded, completely distracted.

"Oh, my dear! How very, very unfortunate! And I've paid for my tickets, or I might have been able—Oh dear, I wish I weren't going away, but Mary made me promise— you know how unselfish she was, and she thought it would take my mind off. She'd been an invalid so long, and of course that is always a strain, and she made me promise that as soon as I could after the funeral I would go right away—and when Peter told me about this cruise—"

"I know. Dear Cousin Lucy, do listen. I should hate you not to go for your cruise."

"She made me promise," said Miss Lucy with a sob. "But I don't really feel I ought to go, because—oh, my dear, you know Ross is turning me out."

It was Lee's turn to gasp. She said, "No!" and Miss Lucy said, "Oh, he is!" and gave another and a much louder sob.

"Ross Craddock is turning you out? Cousin Lucy, he *can't!*"

"He says he can. He says there was nothing in the will. He says he wouldn't turn Mary out, but now she's gone he wants to throw the three flats into one, and he says I'm quite able-bodied. He says I've got to go. I got the letter this morning."

Lee stamped her foot so hard that she jarred the line.

"What a swine!" she said, and shocked Miss Lucy a good deal.

"Oh, my dear, I don't think—"

"Well, I do! What put him up to it?"

Miss Lucy's voice trembled.

"He says he wants the whole floor to himself—dear Mary's flat, and his, and mine—and to throw them all into one. He says he wants more room. But I think it's because I spoke to him about Mavis—I do indeed. He was so angry, and told me to mind my own business, but after all she *is* my niece, and I told him it wasn't right and he was getting her talked about. And this morning I got his letter—such a horrible, cruel letter—"

Lee said, "Swine!" again, then added hastily, "What an ass Mavis is!"

"Oh, my dear!"

"She always was. But Ross Craddock—what on earth— she can't like him!"

"Oh, I don't know—he is a very handsome man. I feel I oughtn't to go away, but I *promised* Mary—"

"Of course you must go."

Miss Lucy sniffed.

"To stay here and keep on meeting Ross in the lift and on the stairs—I feel I really can't! I feel as if I should do something before, and it's so very uncomfortable. It's not just because he wants to turn me out. There's Mavis—she's so young—and there are reasons—" Miss Lucy became very much agitated. "I have got quite a desperate feeling—I have indeed. And Peter says it would be better for me to go away."

"Much better," said Lee firmly. "And look here, darling, let's get down to brass tacks. Can I have Cousin Mary's flat?"

Miss Lucy's agitation became less tearful. She said in a flustered voice,

"Oh, no, dear, you can't—Peter's there."

"Peter? Living there?"

"Yes, dear. He is the executor. He is going through all

the papers. Dear Mary never destroyed anything. There are boxes and boxes and boxes of them.''

''Bother! Then that's a wash-out. Well, what about your flat? That's a bright thought, isn't it? I'll keep it aired and warm and beautifully clean, and I won't let Ross so much as cross the threshold. If he tries anything on whilst you're away, there'll be murder done. I can't say fairer than that—can I?''

''My dear—''

''Now, darling, step on it, or you won't catch that train! Listen! I'll be at the barrier. Is it the Folkestone train—the seven-thirty-three? It is? All right, I'll be there. You can bring the keys along and press them into my hand. And you'd better just murmur to Rush that I'm moving in. You needn't bother about Peter—I'll break the news myself.''

Miss Lucy was heard to draw a breath that was almost a gasp.

''Oh, Lee—I don't know if you ought—if I ought—so many people away, and no one on this floor except Ross and Peter—''

''Darling, I've never had a chaperon in my life. Now hurry, hurry, hurry! And *don't* forget the keys!''

CHAPTER
IV

L EE PAID HER taxi and ran up the steps of Craddock
House. It was a very hot evening and the sun fell
scorching on the steps and on her back. All the trains
had been hot, and the station like an oven on baking-day.
She thought lovingly about getting into a large cold bath and
wallowing there.

Rush came up out of the basement with a highly
disapproving air. If he was really going to disapprove of her
having Cousin Lucy's flat, life wasn't going to be worth
living. She cast hastily about for a scapegoat—or goats.
Since he disapproved of nearly everyone in the house, she
led off with affectionate enquiries about the occupants of the
other flats.

By the time they had got her luggage upstairs she had
managed most successfully to divert his attention from
herself. Most of the flat-holders were holiday-making, and
Rush didn't hold with all these goings and comings.

"What people want to go away for when they could stay
'ome and be comfortable beats me all to blazes. Not my
place to call them silly fools, but nobody can stop me
thinking it. There's Lady Trent out of number six—where's
she gone? You've got something mortal 'eavy in this case,
Miss Lee. Abroad, that's where she is, and seventy-five if
she's a day and seventeen stone if she's a hounce. Why

can't she sit quiet at 'ome and see her doctor if she wants company? And Connells out of number five—gone hiking they have—next to nothing on their backs and their knees showing in them shorts. Not my idea of what's decent in a young married lady. And Potters away out of ten and eleven—seaside for the children. And number two's away, and number three, and your aunt—''

"Cousin," said Lee.

Rush snorted.

"Aunt's what she looks like! Sea-voyaging she's gone, and sick she'll be if what she's like in the lift's anything to go by. Twenty-five years she's been going up and down in it and she's never got over saying 'Oh!' and a-clasping of herself. Is it bricks you've got in 'ere may I ask, miss?''

"Books," said Lee.

Rush banged the case down at the foot of Miss Lucy's bed.

"They're pretty well all away," he said. "Mr. Ross, he's in number eight, and Mr. Peter Renshaw's in number nine a-tearing up of your Aunt Mary's papers."

Lee murmured "Cousin," and got a baleful glare.

"Your Aunt Mary's papers," said Rush firmly. "And Miss Bingham in number twelve, she come back yesterday. And number one's here—Mr. Pyne, he don't go away, not much he don't."

"Well, that's nice for you," said Lee kindly.

Rush straightened up. He was a sturdy, square old man with a close-cut grey beard and a bright, belligerent eye.

"Look here, Miss Lee, I don't want none of that," he said. "What's in my job I'll do, and what's in other people's jobs I'll see to it that they do, or the worse for them, but that there Pyne in number one, do you know what he arst me to do no further back than yesterday? 'Rush,' he says, 'your boots is that 'eavy they jar my nerves. Couldn't you wear slippers in the 'ouse?' he says. Laying back in his chair he was, with smelling-salts in his 'and. And I says, 'I could, Mr. Pyne, but I ain't going to. It ain't part of the job,' I says. What's he think I am—sick-nurse or summat?''

He gave a short angry laugh.

Lee had an entertaining vision of Rush in a starched cap. She said consolingly,

"Well, you've still got Mr. Pyne, and this floor's full— me in here, and Ross in number eight, and Peter in number nine. Quite a nice little family party, aren't we?"

Rush stumped out of the room into the hall.

"I've not got nothing against Mr. Peter," he said. "Mr. Ross, he'll go too far one of these days."

Ross seemed to have been making himself popular. Rush grumbled at everyone, but there was something harsher than a grumble in his voice now.

She said lightly, "Don't start quarrelling with your bread and butter," and saw the old man fling round with a jerk.

"Bread and butter?" he said. "That's all some folks think about! There's time I feel as if Mr. Ross's bread 'ud choke me, and I'll be telling him so one of these days—or choking *him*."

In spite of the heat a little cold shiver ran over Lee. The outer door of the flat stood half open, and as she shivered she heard a step go by. It went past, and it stopped. A latch clicked, a door banged. Lee ran across and shut her own.

"Oh, Rush, how stupid you are!" she said in a scolding voice. "Why do you want to say things like that at the top of your voice for everyone to hear? If that was Ross, what's the odds he heard what you said? You've torn it properly!"

The old man stood there glowering.

"It might be Mr. Ross or it mightn't. How do I care what he heard? Didn't I say I'd be telling him one of these days? If he goes too far, he goes too far. And if he heard what I said, he's welcome!"

"Why are you so angry with him? What's he been doing?"

Rush elbowed her away from the door in his rudest and most determined manner.

"Nothing I'd be likely to talk about to you!" he said, and went stumping out, and down the stairs.

She could hear him muttering to himself all the way to the next flight. She wondered more than ever what Ross had done to offend him. Of course it was very easy to offend

Rush. He had been porter there for thirty years, and considered that the place belonged to him. He remembered John Peter Craddock, and he had served John David. The present owner had never been anything more than Mr. Ross, and if he disapproved of Mr. Ross he could see no reason why he shouldn't say so.

Ross wouldn't be so stupid as to take it seriously—Ross couldn't. But Ross was turning Cousin Lucy out. If he could do that . . .

Lee frowned and went to shut the door, but before she could do anything about it there was a knock and a deprecating cough. Instead of shutting the door she opened it, and beheld the limp, dejected form of Mrs. Green.

Twenty years ago Mrs. Green would have been described as a char. Now she aspired to the title of caretaker, but after one severe trouncing from Rush at the beginning of her engagement three months previously she had had to fall back upon the useful compromise of daily help. She scrubbed the stairs and cleaned the lift, very inefficiently according to Rush, who had been heard to describe her as a snivelling hen. She also "obliged" in several of the flats. She had a lachrymose voice, a good deal of untidy grey hair, and a large port-wine mark all across the left side of her face. In spite of the heat of the day she was shrouded in an old Burberry. A black felt hat of uncertain shape was tipped well over on one side of her head. To the other she clutched a faded blue crochet shawl with a border which had once been white.

Beholding Lee, her mouth fell open.

"Oh, Miss Fenton—"

Lee felt as if everyone in the building was in a conspiracy to prevent her from having that nice cold bath. She prepared to be short with Mrs. Green.

"Oh, Miss Fenton—I thought perhaps I'd just catch Miss Craddock—"

Lee shook her head.

"She's gone."

Mrs. Green leaned against the door jamb. She groaned and shut her eyes.

"What's the matter?"

"I do feel that bad. I was going to ask if I might set down for a minute."

There was nothing for it. Lee stood back without any very hospitable feeling.

Mrs. Green swayed limply to one of the hall chairs and sank down upon it with another groan. A glass of water was not welcomed with any enthusiasm. She touched it with a shrinking lip, and murmured in the manner of one about to swoon,

"If Miss Craddock had a mite of brandy—"

Lee wondered just how bad the woman was, and then scolded herself for being harsh. The brandy sounded suspicious, but under a hastily switched on light Mrs. Green really did look rather ghastly. Lee said with a catch in her breath,

"What is it? Won't you tell me? Shall I call Rush?"

She could have administered no sharper restorative. At the porter's name Mrs. Green's drooping head came up with a jerk.

"Him?" she said. "Why, he hasn't got any 'uman feelings, Rush hasn't—thinks no one can't enjoy bad health except that lazy old lie-abed wife of his." Her voice dropped into a sob. "Oh, miss, you won't tell him. I'll get the sack for sure if you do."

"For being ill?" said Lee.

Mrs. Green sniffed.

"He hasn't got 'uman feelings. Last time I had one of me turns he carried on something shocking. 'And I suppose you think I do it to enjoy myself, Mr. Rush,' I said, and he took and told me that if I did it again I could go and enjoy myself somewhere else. And all I done was arst for the loan of a mite of brandy. 'Just you take a drop of brandy when you get one of your turns, Mrs. Green, and it may be the saving of you.' That's what they told me in the 'orspital. I suppose Miss Craddock hasn't left a drop?"

"I'm sure she hasn't," said Lee.

"Then I'll be getting along," said Mrs. Green in a voice of gloom. "The sooner I get along and into my bed the better, because this isn't only the beginning of it, this isn't. Twenty-four hours my turns last, regular. There isn't nothing you can do for them neither let alone a drop of brandy that eases the pain. Right up in the top of my head it starts, and that violent no one 'ud credit it, not if they hadn't had it like what I have, and down it goes till it's through and through me. Grips my heart something cruel it do, and if I don't get home before it comes to that I'm liable to faint right off. Many's the time I've been picked up and taken home for dead." She heaved a heavy sigh and got to her feet. "I done the stairs this morning. Mr. Rush can say what he likes, but I done them. And Mr. and Mrs. Connell's away, and I've cleaned up after them and no business of Mr. Rush's, and if he's got anything to say about my taking a day off, it's a sinful shame, and I hope there's some that'll speak for me. I wouldn't mind going to Mr. Craddock about it. It's him that's master here, and not that upstart of a Rush, when all's said and done."

"Yes, I should," said Lee, and opened the door.

Mrs. Green paused on the threshold to groan and wreathe the faded shawl about her neck.

"There's a bus I could get if I'd some coppers for it," she said in hollow tones.

Lee gave her sixpence, and was glad to see her go. But when she had shut the door her heart smote her and she thought, "How horrible to be a daily help, and have turns, and go round cadging brandy and bus fares." She wondered if the turns were real, because if they were, perhaps she ought to see Mrs. Green safely back to wherever it was she lodged. She had taken off her dress and turned on the bath, but it came over her that she had been harsh. Supposing she had been a brute to Mrs. Green. Supposing Mrs. Green was swooning on the stairs or being taken up for dead in the street. . . .

Lee put on her dress again and ran down. There was no one to be seen except Rush, who was crossing the hall. He looked so bad-tempered that Lee thought she wouldn't ask him any questions. The big front door stood open. She ran down the steps and glanced up and down the street. A bus had just gone by. With any luck Mrs. Green must have caught it.

She turned back, relieved, to meet Rush's glowering eye.

"I was looking to see if Mrs. Green had gone."

"Want her?" said Rush.

"Oh, no," said Lee.

"Snivelling hen," said Rush.

Lee ran upstairs with a clear conscience, and found the bath running over.

The cold bath was delicious. When it had washed all the clammy, sticky heat away Lee ran some of it off and turned on the hot tap, because even on the most boiling day you can't dally too long in an icy bath, and she wanted to dally. Thank goodness there was a communal hot water supply, very efficiently superintended by Rush, so she wouldn't have to bother about lighting stoves or, what was more important, paying for fuel. She brought the water to a comfortable temperature and wallowed.

A pity about South America, because she had always wanted to go there. Very annoying to have the relations proved perfectly right. Each, every, and all of them had warned her in the most aggravating and aggressive terms.

Warning No. 1—Danger of South America as a destination.

Warning No. 2—Danger of unknown and unpedigreed foreigners as an escort.

And both warnings most lamentably and indubitably justified.

She had got away all right, but there had been one or two horrid moments when she had wondered whether she was going to get away.

Don't be a fool. Stop thinking about it. It's done, finished, dead. And it was Madeleine Deshenka's fault. Of course the relations would rub it in. Relations always did.

She achieved a philosophic calm. Whatever you did they talked, and however it turned out they said "I told you so." Why worry? All the same, Peter Renshaw had better mind his step. The violence of their last quarrel still lingered excitingly in the mental atmosphere. In this very flat, in Cousin Lucy's sitting-room, but during Cousin Lucy's absence, the battle had raged. Lee recalled her own part in it with legitimate pride. She considered that she hurled a very pretty insult. She thought that she had put Peter in his place. If he was going to get uppish just because the Merville man had turned out to be a pig, there would be another really blazing row.

Anyhow Peter would keep. She wasn't going to see him or anyone else tonight. If the telephone bell rang, it could ring itself silly. If anyone came knocking on the door, they could go on knocking until they got bored and went away. Nobody was going to get a chance of saying "I told you so" tonight. Least of all Peter Renshaw. First she would have a long, long, lingering bath, and then she would fry eggs and bacon on the gas stove in the kitchenette, and make toast and tea—she had provisioned herself on the way from the station—and then she would ransack the flat for a really exciting novel and read in bed. Lucy had a taste for thrillers, and with any luck there ought to be something she hadn't read before.

It was over the eggs and bacon that she had a moment of weakness. Bacon and eggs for two are more amusing than bacon and eggs for one, and Peter was only just across the landing. If she were to ring him up. . . . "Idiot!" said Lee. "Do you want to hand yourself over nicely wrapped up in a parcel for him to glory over? And rub it in. And say I told you so. All military and superior. No, you don't, my girl!"

She didn't. She followed out her programme. If she hadn't had so much proper pride, a good many things would have happened differently. Some of them might never have happened at all. But Lee wasn't to know this. She admired her proper pride a good deal, and having eaten her supper sat up against three pillows and read an exciting work entitled *The Corpse with the Clarionet*.

CHAPTER
V

PETER RENSHAW CAME into the Ducks and Drakes and looked about him for the party he had promised to join. If it was stuffy and hot outside in the London streets, it was a great deal hotter and stuffier here. He told himself that it was an act of complete lunacy to go to a night-club in the middle of an August heat-wave. No collar on earth would stand the strain.

He looked across the dancing-floor and saw no sign of the Nelsons. What he did see was Mavis Grey sitting alone at one of the small tables. She had on an extravagantly cut dress cut of some silver stuff. A ridiculous little bag of the same stuff lay on the table beside her. Mavis was looking down at it, playing with the linked handle, snapping the clasp first shut, then open, and then shut again. She had not seen him, and he had no desire to be seen by her. If the Nelsons didn't turn up in five minutes, he meant to be off. In fact the more he thought about it the weaker he felt about giving them as much as five minutes.

Pat on the thought the party arrived—three Nelsons, a sister of Paula's, a brother of Tony's, and a red-haired girl, all hot, all hearty, all game for a couple of hours dancing. His fate was sealed, the collar must take its chance.

He took the floor, first with Paula, and then with the red-haired girl, an artless creature on her first visit to London. She had been sight-seeing hard all day and was full of information about St. Paul's, the National Gallery, and the Houses of Parliament. Peter was able to dance quite peacefully without having to supply any conversation. A vague encouraging sound at remote intervals was all that was required to keep the ball rolling.

Mavis passed them in Ross Craddock's arms—very literally in his arms. His head was bent over hers, and it was he who was doing the talking. Mavis, with her eyes cast down, seemed neither to speak nor to listen. She floated on as if she were in a dream, dark lashes against lovely tinted cheeks, dark hair in a mass of curls caught up with a silver flower. They passed again before the music stopped. This time she lifted her eyes and looked at Peter without surprise, as if she had known all along that he was there. But there was something more in the look than that. It said, "Please, Peter."

Peter Renshaw frowned. If Mavis thought she could run him in a string with Ross Craddock she would have to think again. He wasn't asking for a row with Ross. The fact was, they had never been on very good terms, and the more they saw of one another the worse the terms were likely to be. He gave Mavis an aloof smile, and wondered where Bobby Foster was, and whether Mavis was just playing him up, or what. Perhaps she really liked Ross—there was no accounting for tastes. Perhaps she only thought she liked him because Lucinda kept telling her she mustn't.

He detached himself from a problem in which he felt no particular interest and listened in a faraway manner to the red-haired girl's description of the Tower of London. Her name was Maud Passinger, and she described everything in detail and with immense enthusiasm.

Some time during the next dance he found himself close to Mavis in a jam. She said in her pretty, empty voice,

"Oh, Peter, I never see you."

To which he replied,

"Well, here I am. Take a good long, satisfying look. It costs you nothing."

Mavis's dark eyes opened wide. Her lips parted in a small puzzled smile.

"Well, you know what I mean."

"Not in the least, darling."

"Oh, Peter!"

Paula Nelson was talking heartily to the next couple in the jam.

"Where's Ross?" said Peter.

"He saw a man he wanted to speak to. Peter, aren't you going to ask me to dance?"

"No, my child."

"Oh, Peter—why?"

"Ross appears to have staked out a claim. I am too young to die."

She laughed her tripping laugh at that, and said,

"Silly!" Then, in a patronizing voice, "Are you afraid Ross would hurt you?"

"Perhaps I'm afraid I might hurt Ross."

And with that Paula was saying,

"Aren't we going to dance any more? Do you know who that was that I was talking to? Well, it was a girl I was at school with, and she was so fat we used to call her 'Twice round the Gasworks.' And now look at her. She swears she's only thirty-four round the hips. And that's her husband, and they're over from Kenya, but they'll have to go back again. I do wonder how she's done it. You know, I'd like to be thin, but I just can't be bothered about a diet, and one person tells you nothing but boiled milk, and another says oranges and tomatoes—and I can't bear tomatoes—can you? But perhaps you like them. Such a lot of people seem to, but personally I think they're horrid."

Paula's talk went on and on and on. She had nursed him through a baddish bout of fever, and he felt properly grateful. Beneath the paralyzing dullness of the present moment ran a steady current of affection. He bore up until the party dispersed, and then thankfully retrieved his hat.

A last look back into the room showed him that Mavis and Ross were still together. They were not dancing now, but sitting out under an electric fan. The light just overhead shone through a many-coloured prism upon Mavis's silver dress and the champagne in her glass. Marvellous heads girls had nowadays, but it looked to him as if she had had just about enough. Perhaps a little more. Anyhow it was none of his business.

On the steps he collided with a large young man who said "Sorry," and then clutched him.

"Peter!"

He surveyed Bobby Foster without enthusiasm. The clutch became a bruising grip.

"Peter! Is she still in there?"

Peter's diagnosis was that Bobby had had quite as much to drink as he could carry, and that he was spoiling for a scene. He slipped a hand inside his arm and began to walk away.

"Who is in where?" he enquired soothingly.

Bobby stopped dead and struck an attitude.

"Do you know that she was coming out with me, and when I went to fetch her she'd gone with that—that—"

"I don't know what you're talking about," said Peter, most untruthfully.

A hand like a ham came down upon his shoulder. Most of Bobby Foster's weight appeared to be resting upon it. He swayed on a pair of unsteady legs and said in a broken voice,

"Mavis—he's stolen her—cut in on me and stolen her—I can't give her champagne—like Craddock—"

Peter frowned. He remembered the dazzle of lights on Mavis's glass. What a dratted nuisance girls were. Bobby was a good fellow if a bit of an ass. He couldn't possibly be allowed to go barging into the Ducks and Drakes in the sort of state he was in. A complete toss-up as to whether he would give Ross a black eye or weep on Mavis's shoulder. Either proceeding was bound to create a scandal.

"Look here, Bobby," he said, "it's simply foul in there—Black Hole of Calcutta isn't in it—temperature about ninety-six and still going up. What you want is nice fresh air. You come along with me. If you feel you've got to, you can tell me all about it."

Bobby took no notice.

"I'll knock his head off!" he said in alarmingly loud tones. "Knock it right off and kick it into the gutter!" His voice rose to a bellow. "Shooting's too good for him—that's what I say! The dirty swab! Ouch!" He sprang back with extraordinary agility, managed to retain his balance, and demanded with indignation, "What'd you do that for?"

"It's nothing to what I'll do if you don't stop making such a row."

Mr. Robert Foster nursed his left arm, made several attempts to pronounce the word jujitsu, and fell back upon "Damned dirty trick!"

"Apologize or I won't go another step. Do you get that? Apologize!"

The fact that he could pronounce these four syllables without a tremor appeared to please him so much that he went on doing it.

"You know, if I were you I should go home," said Peter.

"Would you?"

"Yes—and I'd go to bed."

Bobby stared at him with round, blank eyes.

"You'd go home?"

"Yes."

"And go to bed?"

"Yes, I would."

Mr. Robert Foster became suddenly overcome with emotion.

"Ah, but then you haven't lost the only girl you ever loved. And I have. And I've not only lost her, I've had her stolen from me. And by a dirty swab with pots of money. Pots, and pots, and pots of money. And what I say is, shooting's too good for him." He dropped suddenly back into the common-place. "And now I'll go home."

"Yes, I should," said Peter with relief.

Having got Bobby into a taxi before he could change his mind, he continued on his way.

It was a little short of twelve o'clock when he got back to Craddock House. Mary Craddock's Dresden china clock was striking the hour as he came into the flat and shut the outside door with a bang.

CHAPTER
VI

I T WAS MORE than an hour later that he waked with great
suddenness. Waked, or was awakened? For the moment
he wasn't sure, but the more he thought about it the
more it came to him that something had waked him up. He
put on the light and looked about him. The clock made it
half past one.

He got up and looked into the sitting-room. There were
some heavy portraits there. One of them might have fallen.
That was the impression that he had brought with him out of
his sleep—a crash—something heavy falling. But old David
Craddock in neckcloth and whiskers still gloomed between
the windows; his wife, Elizabeth, stood stiff in puce bro-
cade; whilst over the mantelpiece his daughters, Mary and
Elinor, in white muslin and blue ribbons, played with an
artificial woolly lamb.

He went back to the bedroom and listened. He could hear
nothing, but that impression of having heard some loud and
unfamiliar sound was very strong. The bed stood with its
head against the wall which separated this flat from the next.
Ross Craddock's sitting-room lay on the other side of it. If
something had crashed in that room it might very easily
have waked him from his sleep.

A crash—yes, that was what it had been. The impression
was getting stronger all the time. He hesitated for a mo-

ment, and then went to the outer door and opened it. A light burned on the landing all night long. Rather a dingy light, but sufficient to show him the empty lift-shaft, two flights of stairs, one up, one down, and the perfectly bare landing with Lucy Craddock's door facing him across it, and Ross Craddock's door on his right facing the entrance to the lift. There wasn't the slightest sound of anything stirring. The whole great block might have been uninhabited except for himself.

He was just stepping back, when the door of Ross's flat was wrenched open and Mavis Grey ran out. Her silver dress was torn. She tripped and stumbled over it as she ran, and it tore again. Before Peter had any idea what she was going to do she had flung herself into his arms, and before he had time to say more than "What on earth—" Ross Craddock stood in the open doorway staring at them.

He stared, and he stood there swaying as if he were drunk. Peter thought he was drunk. And there was Mavis shuddering in his arms. He said,

"Look here, hold up. What's happened?"

She was clutching him and sobbing violently.

"Oh, Peter! Oh, don't let him touch me!"

Peter said, "It's like that, is it? What have you done to her? Mavis, pull yourself together. Has he hurt you?"

"Of course I haven't," said Ross.

He laughed in a confused sort of way. He had one hand on his head. He dropped it now and held it out palm upwards. The palm was darkly stained. Blood ran down his face from a cut above the eye. He laughed again and said heavily,

"I was the one that got hurt."

"Well, we can't have a scene about it here," said Peter. "Come in if you've anything to say."

Mavis sobbed and clung to him.

Ross said, "Thank you, I've had enough." He stood there and watched them, swaying.

Peter stepped back and banged his door. He was in a state of pure rage. This *would* happen as soon as Lucy had gone away. And a bit of pure luck if no one had heard Mavis sob.

She had made enough noise over it in all conscience. He removed her arms from about his neck, put her firmly into Mary Craddock's big armchair, and said,

"You'd better tell me what's happened."

Mavis let her head fall back against the magenta cushion and closed her eyes.

"Something to drink—" she said faintly.

Peter brought her cold water. She revived sufficiently to register indignation.

"I don't call water something to drink!"

"If you'd stuck to the water-wagon you wouldn't be here tonight," said Peter grimly.

Mavis shuddered. She was suddenly young and disarming.

"You don't seem to notice what a lot you're drinking when everyone's doing it too, but it does make you do things you wish you hadn't afterwards—doesn't it?"

"It has been known to."

She leaned forward.

"But I wouldn't have come here tonight if I'd known Aunt Lucy had gone—oh, Peter, I really wouldn't. He said she'd put off going—something to do with business. And he said it was so late, why not come back here and get her to put me up? Because the Greys do fuss most frightfully if I'm not in before twelve. And I didn't know she'd gone till I got here, and then he said he'd made a mistake."

"It's the sort of mistake he'd be likely to make—isn't it?"

Mavis looked puzzled.

"I don't see how he could. Do you? Not really. I mean he couldn't have thought she had put off going unless she had told him so herself—I mean there couldn't have been any mistake. And anyhow everyone always knows everything that's going on in these flats."

Peter looked piously at the ceiling.

"Let's hope, my dear, that everyone doesn't know what's been going on tonight."

"Oh!" said Mavis on a shocked breath. And then, hopefully, "But they're nearly all away, aren't they?"

"Miss Bingham came back last night, and she's the worst of the lot."

"She told Aunt Lucy I wanted watching," said Mavis, with a faint hysterical giggle.

"And I'm sure she'd have been most happy to oblige."

"Oh, Peter!"

"Oh, Mavis!"

She shivered and sat up.

"What had I better do?"

"Let me take you home, I imagine."

She looked over her shoulder at the clock.

"Oh, Peter—is that right?"

"Absolutely. It's a quarter to two."

"Then I can't possibly go home. You don't know what they're like. Aunt Gladys is bad enough, but Uncle Ernest is ten times worse. I mean, Aunt Lucy's a fuss, but she simply isn't in it with the Grey relations."

"All the same I think you will have to go home."

"Peter, I can't—honest. You see, they don't approve of Ross, and they've forbidden me to go out with him, and—well, they think I was at the party at Hampstead with Bobby Foster—his sister Isabel's party—and I rang up from the Ducks and Drakes and said Isabel was keeping me for the night, so you see I simply can't go home."

With rage in his heart Peter saw. He said in a most unpleasant voice,

"What you want is about ten of the best with a hair-brush."

"How can you be so unkind!"

There was a pause. Peter mastered a desire to shake her and said,

"Are you going to tell me what happened? You needn't if you don't want to, but I think you'd better."

Mavis brightened. Now that she wasn't frightened any more there was something exciting about having had such an adventure. And she had always liked Peter much better than Peter had seemed to like her. Perhaps this was an opportunity. He found a little scrap of a handkerchief and dabbed her eyes with it.

"Well, I really *was* going to Isabel's party with Bobby, so I didn't tell a lie about that. But then we quarrelled—"

"You and Bobby, or you and Isabel?"

"Oh, Bobby of course—about Ross. You know, Peter, it's frightfully stupid of people to go on warning you about someone. Everyone has been warning me about Ross for months—Aunt Gladys, and Uncle Ernest, and Aunt Mavis, and Aunt Lucy. You know—all the sort of people you can't have rows with. So when Bobby started in I just let him have it. I'd got it all saved up, and out it came. And then of course I couldn't go to the party with him—could I? So I rang Ross up. Every time any of the aunts do any of their awful warnings I always ring him up—it just makes me feel I must. So I told Bobby I wasn't ever going to speak to him again, and I met Ross at the end of the road."

"Chapter one," said Peter. "And chapter two is fun and games at the Ducks and Drakes, and we can skip that, because I was there and saw most of it. And now we come to chapter three."

Mavis showed some slight embarrassment.

"Well, we got here—"

Peter nodded.

"I'd gathered that."

"And when we got here he said, 'Come in and have a drink,' and I said it was too late, but he said oh, he'd just remembered that Lucy wasn't here after all. And I said, 'Do you mean the flat is empty?' and he said 'Yes,' and a lot about being awfully sorry and all that—and, Peter, I thought he really *was*. And when he said I must come in and talk about what would be the best thing to do, I never thought—honest, Peter, I never thought about there being anything wrong—I really didn't."

"Evil is wrought by want of thought as well as want of heart," intoned Peter.

"How horrid of you! I can't think why no one ever warns me against you. I think you're quite the horridest person I know."

"You'd better go on with chapter three."

He could see her warming to it. Her colour had come back, and her eyes had brightened.

"We went into the sitting-room, and there was a decanter and glasses on the table, and I said I wouldn't have anything more, and he said I must, so he got a bottle of champagne and poured out a glass for me and a glass for him, but I really only sipped it. And then he began to make love to me, and at first I liked it, and then I didn't. And then he got rough, and my dress got torn and I got awfully frightened, and I picked up the decanter and hit him with it as hard as I could, and the table went over and everything broke."

"I heard it. Continue."

Mavis shuddered enjoyably.

"Oh, Peter, I thought I'd killed him. He went right down, and he groaned."

"Dead men don't groan."

"Oh, no, he wasn't dead. I only thought he was. I felt absolutely frozen, but when he began to get up I ran away—and oh, Peter, you can't think how glad I was to see you."

"The pleasure was far from mutual," said Peter, in his most disagreeable voice. "Mavis, you really are an absolutely prize, champion idiot. Anybody could have told you what Ross was like."

"They did tell me," said Mavis tearfully. "That's why I did it."

"That's why I said you were a prize, champion idiot. Now sit up and pay attention and listen. You'll have to stay here tonight."

"Thank you, Peter."

"I don't want you to thank me—I want you to listen. You will stay here tonight. You can have the bedroom, and I'll camp down in here. In the morning you must go to this Isabel woman and tell her the exact truth and get her to back you up. She can lend you some clothes to go home in. And now you'd better try and get some sleep."

"I don't think I can sleep," said Mavis.

"Well, I can," said Peter. "So off you go!"

When she had got as far as the door she turned back.

"Suppose I had killed Ross—" she said rather breathlessly.

Peter was arranging a pile of cushions on the sofa.

"You didn't, worse luck."

Her dark blue eyes opened to their very widest.

"Would you have liked me to?"

"It might have been inconvenient. Pleasant things very often are."

Mavis said, "Oh!" She looked mournfully at her torn dress. "It's quite spoilt, and some of the champagne dripped on it. But I'm glad I didn't kill him. Would it have been murder if I had?"

Peter gave a short enraged laugh.

"If you don't want to be murdered yourself, go to bed and stay there! You'll have to be up again at six or so."

"Why?"

"I suppose you really haven't got any brain. Do you want Miss Bingham to see you, or Rush, or that dreep of a charwoman? . . . No? Then you'll have to get up bright and early and avoid them."

Mavis trailed her torn dress through the doorway between the sitting-room and the bedroom. She said, "I think you're very unkind," and ended on a sob and banged the door.

Peter finished arranging his pile of cushions, switched on the light, and went to sleep. The last thing he heard was the clock striking two.

CHAPTER
VII

IT WAS PETER'S habit to sleep deeply and dreamlessly until (a) somebody waked him—and it took a bit of doing—or (b) an alarm clock went off in his ear. The alarm clock was in the bedroom, and it would go off in Mavis's ear at six o'clock, because he had intended to go out and swim before breakfast. And at six o'clock of an August morning it was broad daylight. So when he waked up a second time in the dark he felt very much annoyed. Not a single gleam of light came through the two open and uncurtained windows. It was stiflingly hot, and the cushions smelt of feathers dust and dye, and he had a crick in his neck.

He got up and stretched himself, and as he did so he heard the latch of the outer door click home. Peter could move very quickly. He was hot, stiff, and sticky, but he reached the hall and had the light on all in a flash. There was a scurry and a scream, and there was Mavis at the bedroom door. But she wasn't coming out. She was trying to get in—and hide. She was still in her silver dress and her silver shoes. She had one hand at her throat, and in the other she clasped the little silver bag which he had seen lying beside her on a table at the Ducks and Drakes. Her eyes stared with fright and all her colour had gone.

"What do you think you're doing?" said Peter in a rasping voice.

She kept on staring. Her tongue came out and touched her lips. She said in a whisper,

"N-nothing."

"Why did you go out of the flat?"

She moistened her lips again.

"I didn't."

"Have it your own way, but I heard you come in."

She let go of her throat and caught at the door jamb.

"I dropped my bag. It's got all my money. I went to look for it."

"Back to Ross's flat?"

"N-no. I didn't. It was on the landing."

"Where?"

"Just by the door. It's got all my money. I didn't mean to wake you."

"I'm sure you didn't. Are you going out again?"

"N-no, Peter." She took her hand suddenly from the jamb and retreated.

"Then go to bed and stay there!"

Mavis shut the door with alacrity. How awful of him to wake up like that—how perfectly awful!

She put the silver bag down on Aunt Mary's bow-fronted chest of drawers with the ivory escutcheons. Then, as she turned away, she caught sight of herself in the long mirror on the opposite wall. She half cried out, and stood a long time with her eyes fixed.

At last she moved. She looked down, and began to tremble. It wasn't a trick of the light. It was really there—a red soaked patch just under her left knee. How horrible!

She caught up the silver stuff and held it away from her. The stain was about two inches across. Not so very large—and the dress was torn already.

She went over to the dressing-table. There would be nail-scissors—Peter was bound to have a pair of nail-scissors—and she could cut the stain out and nobody would know. Unless Peter . . . But the jamb had been on her left and she had been leaning up against it—and why should he look down at her knee? Oh, he wouldn't—

She had to cut away more than she expected, because the blood had smeared and spread. Then she stood with the piece of stuff in her hand and wondered what she was going to do with it. She didn't dare open her door again in case Peter was listening.

She found matches on the mantelpiece, and used the whole box before she could persuade the heavy, wet stuff to burn. Even so some of the little tinsel threads were left, but she pushed them right away under the grate, and felt sure that no one would notice them there. Then she stripped off the ruined dress and rolled it into a ball. There were still some of Aunt Mary's clothes in the flat, and she would just have to find something that would cover her up until she could get to Isabel. It didn't matter now. Nothing mattered except that she was here and she was safe.

She kicked off her shoes, lay down on the bed, and went fast asleep.

The Dresden china clock on the sitting-room mantelpiece struck three.

CHAPTER
VIII

LEE FENTON OPENED her eyes with a sense of coming back from a very long way off. She had been so deeply asleep that just for a moment her mental focus was out and she did not know where she was. There was an open window on her left with the morning light streaming in, the light of another hot and airless day. There was a fireplace straight in front of her, and over the mantelpiece the enormously enlarged photograph of old Cousin Andrew Craddock, Cousin Lucy's father.

With that it came back to her that she was in Lucy's bed, in Lucy's room, in Lucy's flat. She became a little wider awake and pushed away the sheet, which had got tucked up under her chin. There was a most extraordinary weight upon her spirits—a horrid sense that something had happened, and that in about a half a minute she was going to remember what it was. She pulled herself up in bed and stretched. It wasn't the Merville man. There had been some nasty moments, but she had got away and could afford to snap her fingers. It was not Miss Fenton's habit to hang shuddering over an unpleasant might-have-been.

She sat up frowning. A dream—that was what it was. She had had a perfect beast of a dream, and some of the nightmare feeling was still hanging around. She couldn't remember the dream, but it must have been a particularly bad one for her to feel like this. She threw the sheet right off her, swung her legs over the edge of the bed, and stayed there staring, with a hand on either side of her, pressing down hard upon the mattress and the old linen sheet which covered it. The hem of her pale pink nightgown was stained a handsbreadth deep with blood . . . and her right foot too.

Just for a moment the black curtain which hid her dream trembled and grew thin. From behind it came somebody's voice crying out in a frightened way.

The curtain thickened and darkened again. She was looking at the blood on the hem of her nightgown, and at her blood-stained foot. All at once she jumped up. The nightgown fell round her to her feet. The stain ran right across the front of the hem, but broader on the right-hand side, as if she had stepped on it with that stained right foot.

She made a little sound of disgust and ran out of the room and across the hall to the bathroom. She washed her foot, and threw the nightdress into cold water to soak.

It was when she was coming back that she saw the blurred print of her foot on the threshold of the room where she had slept. She found her dressing gown and put it on, and then went back to switch on the hall light. The prints ran all across the hall from the front door to the threshold of Cousin Lucy's room. When she stooped down and looked closely she could trace them across the Turkey carpet to the bed.

She stood by the front door for a long time before she opened it. There were the prints again, running straight from the door of No. 8 to the door of No. 7—straight from Ross Craddock's flat to the one where she had slept—and dreamed a horrible dream.

She went back into the flat, took a pail of water and a swab, and washed the prints away, first the ones on the landing, and then, very carefully, the ones inside the flat. She poured the water away, and rinsed the bucket, and washed the swab quite clean before hanging it up to dry. The sheets were stained. She wondered what she should do about them. You can't wash sheets in a flat. At least, you can wash them, but you can't get them dried and ironed—

not in time. In time for what? Rush was an early riser. If he came stumping up the stairs. . . . Well, let him come—she had washed the landing clean. But behind the door of No. 8—behind Ross Craddock's door—She cut her thoughts short. The door was shut, the door was locked. There was nothing to do about it. Get on with the things which have to be done here.

She took the sheets into the bathroom and sponged out all the stains. She hung them over a couple of chairs by the open window to dry. They wouldn't take long on such a hot morning. Whilst they were drying she had a bath and dressed herself.

All this time she hadn't let herself think. When there wasn't anything more to do she found that her knees were shaking. She sat down on the edge of the bed, and all the things which she had been trying not to think about came rushing into her mind. Something dreadful had happened. It would come back to her out of that dream which she couldn't remember. She had wandered in a horror of darkness, and in that darkness something dreadful had happened. She did not know what it was. The black curtain hid it, but presently she would know.

The thought terrified her. She tried to think how much longer that shut door of No. 8 would remain shut. Ross employed a man to valet him and keep his flat. He came in by the day. She began to wonder how soon he would come. Not before seven, she thought. She supposed he would have a key. Well, then, he would open the door and go in. . . . She got no farther than that. Her mind felt numb and blank.

She went into the kitchen and looked at the clock, an old eight-day wall-clock with a heavy tick. You could see it the moment you opened the door. The short hand stood at five, and the long was very near to the half hour. But she remembered that it was fast, so it was really only five o'clock. Cousin Lucy was always talking about having it regulated, but the clock had been half an hour fast for at least ten years, and would probably go on being fast to the end.

When the sheets were dry she put them back on the bed,

tumbling and crumpling them so that the washed places should not show. It was now about a quarter to six. She opened the flat door and looked out. Rush was moving down below. She could hear him sweeping the hall. She ought to put a note out for the milkman. It was extraordinarily stabilizing to think about things like the milkman coming, and having to go round to the shops for groceries. She tried hard to keep her mind on groceries and the milkman.

It was no use, she couldn't do it. Her eyes went to that shut door, and her thoughts went too. She couldn't take her eyes away, and she couldn't stop her thoughts. There is a dreadful sort of nightmare in which you can't run away and a pursuing something is coming nearer, nearer, nearer. But this was worse, because she couldn't even stand still. The thing behind that shut door was drawing her—her eyes, her shuddering thoughts. With a frantic effort she dragged them away and ran across the landing to the door of No. 9. Peter—she must get to Peter—then perhaps she would wake up and find it was all a terrifying dream. The quarrel on which she had dwelt with so much satisfaction last night had dwindled to a speck. Peter was Peter, and if she could get to him, everything would be all right.

She rang the bell, and waited with an agonized fear lest he should be away. Her finger went again to the bell, as if its persistent ringing must reach him wherever he was and call him back. But when the door opened and she saw him she was suddenly calm. She said, "I want to come in," and stepped past him into the hall.

If it had been anyone but Lee, the door would not have been opened widely enough to let the visitor in. But Lee— Lee who was on her way to South America with a damned dago. . . . No, thank God, she wasn't—she was here.

Peter opened the door so that there should be no mistake about it, and Lee was inside and the door shut again. He said, "Lee!," and she said, "Peter!" and he put his arms round her and said, "Darling!" And what Lee would have said to that he wasn't to know, because at that moment the bedroom door opened and Mavis Grey came out. She was wearing the late Miss Mary Craddock's best thin summer dress, a dark grey silk with a pattern on it of mauve forget-me-nots and black leaves, and at any other time her appearance in this incongruous garment with its shapeless bodice and its long, full skirt, would certainly have made Lee and Peter laugh. At the moment their reactions were of a different nature.

Peter said "Damn!" very heartily, and Lee released herself with a jerk. This was natural enough. It was Mavis whose behaviour was surprising. She stared at Lee, and all the colour went out of her face. Left high and dry, the brightly painted lips were in abrupt and shocking contrast with its pallor. She gave a faint sobbing cry and stammered out words which made no sense.

"You—I thought—oh!"

Lee had turned very nearly as pale. She went back until she came to the wall, and leaned there.

Mavis put out a groping hand and fell.

CHAPTER

IX

MAVIS'S SWOON WAS sufficiently prolonged to be alarming. They got her on to the bed, and after a while she came round and began to cry in a hysterical manner. It was manifestly impossible to take her down two flights of stairs and along to the end of the street, whence Peter had proposed to despatch her in the direction of Isabel.

It was upon Peter that her eyes first rested. She said with a choking gasp, "I thought I saw Lee Fenton." To which he returned with some grimness, "You did."

It was after this that the hysterical weeping came on. The sight of Lee seemed to make her so much worse that Miss Fenton, not unwillingly, retired to the sitting-room. She was immediately followed by the indignant Mr. Renshaw.

"Look here, Lee—"

"You'd better go back to her, hadn't you?"

"I'm damned if I'll go back!"

"You can't leave her alone."

"Well, I'm not going to be alone with her."

"You appear to have been alone with her all night," said Lee with stiff, strange lips. Her eyes were a stranger's eyes. They looked upon Mr. Renshaw for the first time, and found him a displeasing sight.

Peter was appalled.

"Lee, you can't possibly think—"

"What am I to think?"

Peter ran both hands violently through his hair. He then gripped her wrists.

"Woman, do you want to hear me swear?"

"You have been swearing," said Miss Fenton loftily, but her heart was extraordinarily lightened. This was not the language of conscious guilt.

The grip on her wrists tightened painfully.

"It's nothing to what I can do if you get me going. No, look here, Lee, don't be a fool. You're not one really, and only a blithering, blasted little fool could possibly imagine what you're pretending to think."

"Mavis—"

"Mavis gives me a pain in the neck—she always has, and she always will."

"Ssh! The door's open."

"I'd like to shout it from the housetops!" said Peter, with ferocity. "I've never had any use for her. And she's just ruined my night's rest, and butted in when I was going to kiss you."

He let go of her wrists suddenly and put his arms round her, but she pushed him away.

"No! Oh, Peter—no! I didn't come for that. You mustn't— we mustn't. Something dreadful has happened."

It was not so much the words that gave him pause. There was an urgency in her voice and in the thrust of her hands. He took fright and said roughly,

"Not to you! My God—not to you!"

She said, "Oh, Peter, I don't know. Oh, Peter, help me!"

"It isn't that man—that damned dago?"

"No—no—oh, no."

His face cleared.

"What do you want to frighten me like that for? What's the matter? What's happened?"

She caught his arm.

"Peter, that's just it—I don't know."

"But you said 'something dreadful.' "

"Yes—it was—it must have been—but I don't know what." She was shaking all over, and the words shook too.

He got her over to the sofa, made her sit down, and piled three cushions at her back. Then he took her hands and said, "Tell me."

She had wondered whether she would be able to, but the words came with a rush.

"Something dreadful has happened in Ross Craddock's flat."

He got up then, went quickly to the door which communicated with the bedroom, and shut it. Mavis was still crying, but quite softly now. He came back to Lee.

"Sorry, darling. You were saying something had happened in Ross's flat. What makes you think so?" He had her hands again, and he felt them tremble.

"Peter, you know, after the accident—when my father and mother were killed—I used to walk in my sleep. They said it was because of the shock. They said I would stop doing it—and after a time I did. I was about fifteen."

Peter began to be afraid again. He held her hands very tight. She went on, breathing quickly and trying to control her voice.

"I'd had a long journey. The Merville man really was a damned dago, and I had to come away in a hurry. I just caught Cousin Lucy, and she gave me her key. She said I could have the flat whilst she was away. Well, I was all in. I went to bed and read a thriller. Then I went to sleep. It had all been rather beastly—and what with that, and being so tired—I—well, I suppose I must have walked in my sleep again."

"How do you know?"

She turned very pale indeed.

"Because when I woke up—"

"Go on."

"It was my foot," she said in a whisper—"my right foot—as if I had stepped—in blood—all stained—and the hem of my nightgown too. And the mark of my foot all across the hall. And when I opened the front door it was all across the landing—all the way from Ross's flat."

Peter threw back his head and laughed.

"My poor child! Did you think you'd done murder? Look here, it's all right—quite all right. Listen. There's a perfectly simple explanation. The idiot Mavis allowed herself to be lured into Ross's flat last night. She said she didn't know Lucy was going to be away—meant to spend the night there, and walked into Ross's parlour to discuss alternatives. Ross got fresh. She hit him over the head with one of the ancestral decanters and staggered out on to the landing. The crash having waked me, I was there. She cast herself upon me, and I had to take her in after a few kind words with Ross, who came out of his door in a stoshed condition, bleeding like a pig—cut over the eye. So you see where the gore came from. No need to worry and all that. But I don't like your wandering around in the night. You want someone to look after you, you do."

The blessed, the overwhelming relief brought up a thick mist before Lee's eyes. The room seemed to tilt a little. Peter's voice came through the mist.

"Here, hold up. I can't kiss you if you're going to faint."

CHAPTER

X

THE RELIEF DIDN'T last. It ought to have lasted, but it didn't. She was here in Peter's arms. She was safe. And everything was quite all right. But a cold, deadly fear was seeping back into her mind. She drew away, and Peter came down to earth.

"Look here, we'd better get rid of those footprints before anyone comes."

The fear was in Lee's eyes as she looked at him.

"I did it—I washed everything—at once."

"Practical child! Sure you made a good job of it?"

She was seeing the landing in a horrid sharp picture, with herself on her knees and the wet swab in her hand. But there had only been footprints, nothing but her own footprints. There hadn't been any pool she could have stepped in—not out there, not on the landing. She began to shake again.

"What is it?" said Peter quickly.

"There wasn't any pool, Peter—there wasn't. I washed the landing. There was only the mark of my foot. The first one was close to the door. Don't you see what that means? I must have been inside the flat—and something's happened there—something—"

Peter spoke sharply.

"Stop it! Pull yourself together! Think—was the door open—Ross's door?"

"No, it was shut."

"Sure?"

"Quite sure—quite, quite sure."

"Then how could you have got in? Be reasonable."

She looked at him in a distressed way.

"I don't know. You said Ross was stoshed. Perhaps he didn't shut the door when he went in—if he was drunk. Did you mean that he was drunk?"

"Oh, he'd certainly been drinking, but I don't suppose he was drunk. It takes a lot to make Ross drunk. No, he was just stoshed—silly—didn't know what he was doing. Mavis had knocked him out. A decanter full of whiskey is quite a hearty weapon. Yes, I suppose he might have left the door open, but there's nothing in that to worry you— No, but—by gum, there is! Because if you were inside the flat, those pretty little footprints of yours will be damn well all over the place." He laughed. "It's no odds, because he'll only think it was Mavis, and he'll want to hush the whole thing up. And his man won't know who was there—only that there was a rough house and a lot of mess to clear up. And I don't suppose it's the first time by a long chalk. I expect he's paid to hold his tongue. Now look here, what about this girl Mavis? The best thing we can do now is to cart her across to Lucy's flat, and officially she spent the night there. In fact, you chaperon each other. By the way, I don't know what she was up to, but she went out again after I took her in. She had the bedroom, and I was in here, and I heard the front door. Something had just waked me, and there she was, sneaking in with a little silver bag in her hand."

"What?"

Peter nodded.

"It was hers all right—matched her dress—made of the same stuff. She had it with her at the Ducks and Drakes—"

"You were at the Ducks and Drakes—last night?"

Peter grinned.

"I was, my child, but not with her. She was with our

dear cousin Ross. She had the little silver bag. And I was with the Nelsons and a party.'' He groaned. ''All enthusiastic, up from the country, and the temperature rising ninety! There is no call for jealousy. But to return to Mavis. She said she'd dropped her bag on the landing after the fracas, but I'm prepared to swear she hadn't got it when she came tottering out of Ross's flat, so it looks to me as if she had gone back for it.''

''Would she, if he had frightened her as much as that?''

''That depends on what was in the bag, and how badly she wanted it. She might have reckoned on his being asleep.''

''But she couldn't have reckoned on finding the door open.''

''She might have gone out on the landing to see if she had dropped it there, and then found that the door wasn't shut.''

There was a pause. Lee said in a careful voice,

''It couldn't have been shut. If it had been shut, I couldn't have got in. But if I was walking in my sleep—'' She broke off. ''I wonder which of us shut the door, because it was shut this morning, and one of us must have shut it—either Mavis or I.''

Without waiting for him to speak she turned away. ''We'd better see how she's getting on,'' she said, and went quickly to the communicating door. But no sooner was it open than she turned a frightened face on him.

''Peter—she's gone!''

Peter said, ''Nonsense!'' and, when they had looked in the bathroom and kitchen, ''Good riddance.'' But he was left with a feeling of profound discomfort. Mavis had fainted when she saw Lee, and it was a real honest-to-goodness faint and no sham. And now she had run away without a word to either of them, and though it was a good riddance, it was also a disquieting circumstance.

He went out on the landing and listened. Rush was down in the hall. He could hear him stumping about, swishing with a broom. He had probably seen Mavis, but it couldn't be helped. He returned to his own hall.

"I must go back," said Lee, "before anyone comes. They'll all be coming up and down now—Rush, and Mrs. Green—no, I don't suppose she will, because she had one of her turns yesterday—but there'll be Ross's man—"

He felt her stiffen against his arm.

"He comes about seven," he said.

"Yes," said Lee in a whisper.

CHAPTER
XI

Ross Craddock's man came in at the front door and gave the porter a civil "Good morning, Mr. Rush." He was a quiet, melancholy-looking man in his forties, dark-eyed, dark-haired, and sallow-skinned. "Puts me in mind of an undertaker," Rush used to tell his wife. "And soft on his feet like a cat. Suit Mr. Pyne a treat, he would. Now I say, and I'll hold to it, that a man that is a man, well, he walks like a man—that's what I say. He don't go slipping and sliding as if he didn't want no one to know what he was up to like that there Peterson does, or a prying old maid like Miss Bingham."

Mr. Peterson walked softly up two flights of stairs and crossed the landing without making a sound. He had his latchkey ready, and inserted it with the ease of long practice. The hall was dark. The bathroom and kitchen doors faced him, and they were shut. The sitting-room door, which was on his right, was open, but no light came from it, the velvet curtains being drawn and the room in darkness. The bedroom door on the left was shut. The place reeked of spirits.

Peterson put on the hall light, and was immediately startled out of his accustomed routine. Instead of entering the kitchen he remained where he was, his hand just dropped from the switch and his eyes fixed upon the floor. Mr. Craddock had a soul above linoleum. The floor was of a light parquet, with a yellow and blue Chinese rug laid across it. And across the parquet and the yellow and blue of the rug were the marks of a naked foot printed in blood.

You can't mistake a bloodstain, try how you will. Peterson would have been very glad of anything that would have explained those marks away. If you were own man to a gentleman like Mr. Craddock, there were things you had to put up with, and things that were best not talked about, but you didn't reckon on bloodstained footprints, no, that you didn't.

He went quickly over to the bedroom door, tapped lightly, and looked in. The curtains here were of chintz, and the light came through them, a tempered yellowish light, but enough to show that the bed had not been slept in, that it was in fact as he had left it, neatly turned down, with Mr. Craddock's rather loud pyjamas laid out across the foot. Mr. Craddock's taste in pyjamas was one of the subjects upon which Peterson exercised a wise discretion.

He turned back, still not greatly alarmed, because he had before now found Mr. Craddock on the sofa, or even—though this had only happened once—upon the floor. He switched on the sitting-room light, and for a moment his only thought was that Mr. Craddock had done it again. And done it properly this time. The little table on which he had set out the drinks had been pushed over, and a chair was overturned. Broken glass too—well, that would account for the blood. There'd been a girl here, and she'd cut her foot. Nasty stuff, broken glass. Lord—what a blind it must have been! And Mr. Craddock dead to the world, sprawling there on the floor with the bits of a smashed decanter all about him.

With a slight reproving click of the tongue, Peterson stepped forward. And then he saw the revolver—Mr. Craddock's own revolver, the one he kept in the second drawer of his writing-table. And it lay on the hearth-rug a couple of yards away from Mr. Craddock's outstretched left hand. And Mr. Craddock lay in a pool of blood. Mr. Craddock was dead.

The quiet Mr. Peterson let off a yell and went out of the flat and helter-skelter down the stairs calling for Rush. There was an interval of perhaps two minutes before they returned together, the porter having left the hall and gone down into the basement. By the time they reached the landing the door of Mr. Peter Renshaw's flat was open and he was coming out of it, pulling on a dressing-gown as he came, while Miss Bingham, without her front, was hanging over the banisters half way down from the floor above and demanding in a high, persistent voice,

"What's the matter? Oh dear—what's the matter?"

Behind the door of No. 7 Miss Lee Fenton was wondering how soon she could open that door. Had there been enough noise to wake her, or hadn't there? But if it was a question of waking, she oughtn't to be dressed like this. She heard the sound of hurrying feet, and she heard Miss Bingham scream. She couldn't stand the suspense another moment. She opened the door and came out upon the landing.

The door of Ross Craddock's flat stood wide open. It had been most terrifyingly shut. Now it was most terrifyingly open. It drew her, and she went towards it, and over the threshold and into the hall.

Miss Bingham was in the hall, and for once she had nothing to say. She was leaning against the wall with her hand to her side and a sick, shocked look on her face. Lee went past her to the sitting-room door, where she came face to face with Peter. He said, "Don't come in," but she looked over his shoulder and saw that Rush and Peterson were there. Peterson was over by the writing-table with the telephone receiver in his hand. The ceiling light was on and all the curtains drawn.

Peter said, "Come away, Lee." But how could she come away until she knew what Rush was looking at? He was standing right in the middle of the room, his hands thrust deep in his pockets, staring down at the floor—at someone lying on the floor—at Ross. And Ross was dead.

Of course she had known that all along.

Before Peter could stop her she said in that very clear voice of hers,

"I told you something dreadful had happened."

CHAPTER
XII

MR. CRADDOCK'S SITTING-ROOM had been restored
to decency and order. The official photographer
had come and gone. Everything that could possibly retain a finger-print had been duly examined and a
record taken. The whole official routine had been gone
through. Mr. Craddock's body had been removed to the
mortuary.

Inspector Lamb sat now at Mr. Craddock's writing-table
and fingered a gimcrack scarlet pen.

"How anyone could write with a thing like that!" he said
in a tone of disgust. "Well, it'll be you, not me, Abbott.
And we'd better get on with those statements. It's murder
sure enough, and an inside job by the look it of. We'll have
the manservant first—what's his name—Peterson?"

Inspector Lamb heaved himself out of his chair as he
spoke. Hot—well, he would say it was going to be hot.
Thunder presently as like as not. He was a stout man with a
small, shrewd grey eye and a heavy jowl. Hair growing thin
on the top, but with no grey in it. Very strong black hair.

Young Abbott was a different type. Flaxen hair sleeked
back; tall, light figure; high bony nose, and colourless
lashes. Public school by the look of him. He went out and
came back with Peterson. The man was composed enough,
but his sallow skin shone damp with sweat.

Abbott was now at the writing-table. On the other side of it, the side towards the room, two chairs were placed. The Inspector filled one handsomely. Peterson, when invited to occupy the other, sat down upon its forward edge and betrayed some nervousness. He gave his name as Matthew Peterson, and his age as thirty-eight. He had been with Mr. Craddock six years. He lived out, and came in daily from seven in the morning until—well, it just depended—he'd get away most days by seven in the evening. Mr. Craddock didn't want him about after that. He preferred being private, as you might say.

Questions about Mr. Craddock's habits. "Would you call them irregular?" Peterson didn't think it was for him to say. Did Mr. Craddock drink? Well, he put away a bit, but it wouldn't be very often that you'd see him drunk.

"Was he drunk last night?"

"Not when I left him, sir."

"And that was?"

"A quarter past seven. I laid out his things and set the drinks ready on the small table in here, and he said that would be all, and I went home."

"That was your usual practice?"

"Yes, sir."

"What did you set out in the way of drinks?"

"Decanter of whisky, siphon of soda, bottle of champagne, and two glasses."

Detective Abbott looked up for a moment, then plied, not the scarlet pen, but one of his own.

"Two glasses—eh?" said the Inspector sharply.

"Yes, sir."

"And was that the usual thing?"

"Yes, sir."

"You always left two glasses?"

"Yes, sir."

"And were they always used?"

"Not both of them—only once in a way, sir."

"And were you in the habit of leaving champagne?"

For the first time Peterson hesitated. Then he said,

"No, sir—only when Mr. Craddock said so."

"And he told you to leave it last night?"

"Yes, sir."

"Well, what did you make of that?"

Peterson hesitated again, and was prompted.

"Did you take it to mean that he was expecting a lady?"

"I suppose I did, sir."

"H'm! How much whisky was there in the decanter?"

"It was full, sir."

"Any idea how it got broken?"

"No, sir."

The Inspector shifted in his chair.

"Well now, I want to talk about those footprints you said you saw in the hall."

"I did see them, sir."

"When you first came in?"

"Yes, sir."

"Regular footprints?"

"Oh, yes, sir."

"Wet, or dry?"

"Dry, sir."

"You're sure about that? How can you be sure?"

Peter cleared his throat.

"The light's right overhead, sir, and as soon as I put it on, well, there were the footprints as plain as plain."

"And they were a woman's footprints?"

"That's what I took them to be."

"Well, what's happened to them?"

"I don't know, sir. I came on in here, and when I saw that Mr. Craddock was dead I ran down the stairs for Mr. Rush, and we came back together. And when I come to look for the footprints to show him, well, sir, they weren't there, no more than what you saw for yourself, sir—a couple of smeared places just short of the rug on this side of the hall, and another over by the door, and the stains on the rug the same as I'd seen them the first time."

The Inspector said "H'm!" Then, sharply, "Would you swear you saw those footprints the first time you came up?"

"Yes, sir, I would. It's the truth, sir."

"Would you swear you didn't touch them?"

"Not the way you mean, sir. I don't say I mightn't have stepped on one of them accidental when I ran down for Mr. Rush. It was—well, it was an awful shock, sir. But stepping on a dry stain wouldn't smear it like those footprints was smeared."

"No," said the Inspector. "And now—just how long were you away?"

Peterson looked anxious.

"It's very hard to say when you've had that kind of a shock. I couldn't get down quick enough. But Mr. Rush he wasn't in the hall. He was downstairs making his wife a cup of tea. I had to go down after him."

"Ah!" said the Inspector. "Mrs. Rush is bedridden, so I'm told."

"Yes, sir."

"Ever known her to be out of her bed?"

"Not the six years I've been coming here."

"Well, you went down and told Rush Mr. Craddock was dead, and the pair of you came up together. It wouldn't be less than two minutes you were away, I take it, and it might be as much as three. And the flat door standing open all the time?"

"Yes, sir."

"Well, someone got in and smudged those footprints— that's clear enough. And when you got upstairs you saw Mr. Renshaw coming out of number nine, and Miss Bingham half way down the stairs?"

Peterson said "Yes" again.

In answer to questions about the revolver, he said it was Mr. Craddock's own revolver. Mr. Craddock kept it in the second draw of his writing-table—"That one on the left, sir." No, the drawer wasn't kept locked—never had been so far as he knew. Mr. Craddock told him once that the revolver was loaded. That would be about six months ago. He couldn't say why Mr. Craddock had mentioned it. Asked whether he had ever handled the weapon, he replied, "Oh, no, sir—certainly not, sir."

"Did you see anyone else handle it this morning?"

Peterson coughed.

"I beg your pardon, sir."

"If it's for coughing, you needn't—if it's for not answering what I've just asked you, it's no good. Did you see anyone handle that revolver?"

Peterson cleared his throat and said, "Yes, sir."

"Out with it, man!"

"It was Mr. Renshaw, sir. He came in as it were right behind us—behind Mr. Rush and me—"

"Yes—go on."

"Well, sir, we looked at Mr. Craddock, and he was dead all right. And Mr. Renshaw he says, 'Good God!' and goes down on his knees and takes hold of his wrist. And Mr. Rush says, 'He's gone! Look at the hole in his head!' And then he says to me to look lively and ring up for the police, so I went over to the table and took up the receiver off the telephone. And then I saw Mr. Renshaw had got up. He went across to where the revolver was and he picked it up. And Mr. Rush said very sharp, 'You put that down, Mr. Peter! There's nothing must be touched.' Mr. Renshaw he had the revolver by the handle."

The Inspector frowned.

"I suppose you mean the butt?"

"Well, you know best, sir. He had it in his right hand the way you'd hold it if you were going to fire—at least, that's the way it looked to me. And when Mr. Rush said that, he said, Mr. Renshaw did, 'Quite true, Rush,' and he shifted the pistol into his left hand, taking hold of it by the other end, and he dropped it back on the floor as near as could be where it was before. And Mr. Rush spoke to him very sharp indeed and told him he'd be getting us all into trouble."

The Inspector frowned more deeply still.

"I want to get this quite clear. You say Mr. Renshaw took hold of the revolver first by the butt and then by the barrel?"

"He took hold first one end and then the other."

That concluded the examination of Peterson, and he was allowed to depart.

"Now what did he do that for?" said the Inspector. "A gentleman like Mr. Renshaw—army officer, isn't he?—he knows as well as you and I do that he oughtn't to have touched that revolver. Now, if it had been Peterson that doesn't know the muzzle from the butt—him and his handles!''—here the Inspector snorted—''you'd say he'd lost his head—and not a lot of it to lose either! But Mr. Renshaw, he knows as well as you and me that that weapon would have to be examined for fingerprints, and when he goes plastering his hands all over it—well, Abbott, what do you make of it?''

Detective Abbott spoke in his pleasant public school voice.

''It looks as if he wanted to make sure that there wouldn't be any fingerprints except those Rush and Peterson had seen him make after Craddock was dead.''

The Inspector nodded.

''Meaning he knew something about the fingerprints that were there, and meant to cover them up—his own likely enough. A bold, impudent trick that, and no mistake.''

Young Abbott shook his head.

''I shouldn't think they'd be his own. If he'd shot the man he'd have wiped the revolver and left it in Craddock's hand. He's too cool a card to have left the place shouting murder when there was quite a decent chance of staging a suicide.''

''Bright ideas you have—don't you, Abbott? Makes me wonder where you get 'em from. What do you know about Mr. Renshaw that makes you say he's a cool card? Ever come across him before?''

Young Abbott's face did not change at all. He said,

''Yes, sir. I was wondering whether I'd better tell you.''

''Well, you'd better tell me now.''

''Well, sir, we were at school together for a bit. He's older of course. I—well as a matter of fact, I fagged for him.''

''And you say he's a cool card?''

''Yes, sir.''

''Well, remember you're not fagging for him now. Lord—it's hot!'' He wiped his brow. ''Better have the porter next,'' he said, and settled back into his chair.

The curtains had been drawn, and the sun shone bright

outside. Rush came stumping into the room, his face very red and his back very stiff. He refused to sit down, and delivered all his answers to a point about a foot over the Inspector's head. His name was Albert Edward Rush, his age was sixty-five years, and he had been porter at Craddock House for thirty of them, leaving out the four years he was away at the war.

The Inspector sat up and took notice.

"Served in the war, did you?"

"August nineteen-fourteen to December nineteen-eighteen."

Rush had no sirs up his sleeve for policemen. His war record was dragged from him a word or two at a time. Royal Fusiliers. Three times wounded. Finished up a sergeant. Glad enough to be back at his job. Yes, of course he knew how to fire a revolver. "What d'you take me for—a blinking fool?"

Inspector Lamb laughed.

"No, sergeant. Well now—did you know Mr. Craddock had a revolver?"

Rush wasn't so ready with his answer this time.

"If I did, what about it?"

"Did you? That's the question."

Rush glared.

"And I say, what if I did?"

The Inspector spoke him fair.

"Come, come—there's no need to take it like that. Did you know he had a revolver?"

Rush was not placated.

"I suppose I did," he said in his surliest voice.

"Did you know where he kept it?"

Rush let out his breath with a snort.

"What are you a-hinting at? Everyone knew where he kep' it. He'd leave the drawer open—anyone could see what was inside."

"Did you ever handle it?"

Rush's eyes were hot and angry. His voice rasped.

"What'd I handle it for? Had enough of the mucky things in the war without wanting to handle one of them now! What are you getting at?"

Detective Abbott's colourless eyebrows rose a little, but the Inspector refused to take offence.

"Well, well, you didn't handle it. But you saw Mr. Renshaw handle it, didn't you?"

"Who says I did?"

"That doesn't matter, sergeant. The question is, what do you say about it?"

Rush stood there stiff and scowling. He snapped out,

"He picked it up. I told him he hadn't oughter."

"How did he pick it up?"

"Butt end first, and when I told him off he caught hold of the muzzle and dropped it down where it come from."

"Get that down, Abbott," said the Inspector. "Now that revolver was fired some time last night—some time between one and four in the morning as near as the medical evidence can put it. I want to know if you heard anything that might have been the shot."

"No, I didn't—nobody couldn't down in that basement."

"And you didn't leave the basement?"

"Not before a quarter to six I didn't. I work I do, and when I go to bed I go to sleep."

"So do I," said the Inspector heartily. "Now I want to know about the outer door of this place."

"Anything wrong with that?"

"No, no. But you lock it up at night, I suppose?"

"Yes, I do."

"What time do you lock up?"

"Eleven o'clock."

"And if anyone wants to get in after that?"

"Those that lives here has their keys."

"The door isn't bolted?"

"Of course it ain't!"

"And what time do you open up in the morning?"

"Six o'clock mostly."

"Now, sergeant—this is very important. You locked up last night as usual?"

"Eleven o'clock I locked up."

"And after you locked up no one could get in without a key?"

"I told you that."

"And when you came to open up at six o'clock this morning the door was locked as you left it?"

"Putting words into my mouth, aren't you? What's the game? Want to get me telling lies and catch me out? Because you won't! See? To start with, it was a good bit before six when I come to open up this morning, and to get on with, the door wasn't locked—it was on the jar."

The Inspector leaned forward with a hand on either knee.

"The door was open?"

"No, it wasn't—it was on the jar, like I said."

"It had been unlocked?"

"Seemingly."

"But you're certain you locked it?"

"When it comes to the proper place I'll be taking my Bible oath I locked it."

The Inspector leaned back again.

"If someone wanted to go out after you locked the place up, could they shut that door without being heard?"

A grim smile appeared on Rush's face.

"You'd better ask Mr. Pyne in number one about that. Ten years he's been complaining about the noise that door makes when it shuts."

"Then if anyone wanted to come or go without being heard, they probably wouldn't risk shutting that door. They would, in fact, be inclined to leave it as you found it, on the jar?"

Rust grunted.

"None of my business what they'd do. I locked up, and that I'll swear to."

Detective Abbott wrote this down. The Inspector looked round at him, said, "I'm taking a list of the flat-holders—get it down on a separate sheet so I can have it handy," and turned to Rush again.

"Now, sergeant, just give me all those flats from A to Z."

"They don't run no more than one to twelve," said Rush, with his scowl at its blackest.

The Inspector was not to be moved from his good humour.

"Well, let's have 'em from one to twelve," he said easily.

Stiffly erect, Rush ticked them off.

"Number one—that's Mr. Pyne. Want me to tell you about 'em as we go along?"

"If there's anything to tell."

"They're people," said Rush. "Always something to tell about people, only it don't always get told."

Here at last was a subject on which he would be willing to talk. Lee Fenton could have told the Inspector that.

"Well, Mr. Pyne, he's in number one—old bachelor as thinks himself an invalid—nothing to do but plan whether it's a pill or a powder he'd best be taking next. He's here all the time—bin here ten years. Number two's Mrs. and Miss Tatterley—went away a week ago. Ladies they are. And number three is the two Miss Holdsworths—and they're away—bin away since the beginning of July. And that's the first floor.

"Then second floor. Number five is Mr. and Mrs. Connell—he's a chartered accountant he is, and she's a bit of a girl. They're gone hiking they have—bin away two days. And number four, that's Miss Lemoine—and she's gone away with old Lady Trent out of number six—gone abroad. So that finishes the second floor.

"The third floor's all Craddocks—Miss Lucy Craddock in number seven, Mr. Ross in here, and Mr. Peter Renshaw in number nine that was Miss Mary Craddock's flat until she died three weeks ago. And Miss Lucy, she went off on a foreign cruise yesterday evening, and Miss Lee Fenton she come in with her aunt's key, so it's her that's in number seven now."

"Miss Fenton came in last night?"

"Round about seven-thirty it would be, and Miss Lucy'd bin gone some time, and Miss Lee Fenton she'd got her aunt's key—met her at the station, she said, and come in to stay till Miss Lucy gets back. And Mr. Renshaw, he's settling up Miss Lucy's affairs. Army officer he is, and Miss Mary's executor. That's the third floor.

"Fourth floor. Potters have ten and eleven—Mr. and Mrs. in eleven, governess and three children in ten. They went off to the sea first of August. Number twelve's Miss Bingham. She got back day before yesterday, and we could have done without her. Prying old maid—that's what she is."

Detective Abbott wrote that down. It occurred to him that a prying old maid might very well be the answer to a policeman's prayer.

Rush was giving particulars about Mrs. Green, the charwoman. She hadn't been with them very long, not above three months, when she took over from old Mrs. Postlethwaite who'd had the job for fifteen years. No, she didn't sleep in. She did her work—he wasn't going to say how she did it. Women weren't a morsel of good at their work so far as his opinion went. She'd gone off with a bad turn last night, and he didn't expect to see her, not before the afternoon, if then.

"Drink?" enquired the Inspector.

Rush shook a gloomy head.

"A silly, peter-grievous female," he pronounced.

The Inspector enquired whether she would have a key to the front door, and was told certainly not.

"Well, that's Mrs. Green. Now what other service was there in the house? All these flats—who looks after them? You and Mrs. Green don't do it all?"

Rush scowled.

"Inside the flats is none of my job, except for Mr. Pyne that I made an arrangement with and many's a time I've wished I hadn't. One of the sort you can't please, he is."

"Well, what do the other people do?"

"Some of them does for themselves, like Miss Craddock, and Mrs. Connell, and the Miss Holdsworths, and Miss Bingham. And some of them has daily help, like Lady Trent and the Potters, but they're away, and when they're away the helps don't come—and I see to it that they hands in their keys, for I won't be responsible without."

"Very sound," said the Inspector.

Rush was dismissed.

CHAPTER
XIII

IN LUCY CRADDOCK'S sitting-room Peter Renshaw stood on the black woolly rug before the empty fireplace and mapped out a plan of campaign. Lee, sitting on the arm of the largest chair, was looking, not at him, but out of the window at a patch of hot, hazy sky. There was a very much worn Brussels carpet on the floor, its original tints of mustard and strong pink now mercifully merged in a general shabbiness. The walls, like those in No. 9, were completely covered with pictures—water colours, etchings, photographic enlargements, and a family portrait or two in oils. There were at least six small tables as well as an upright piano, and a good many unnecessary small chairs. The top of the piano was quite covered with photographs in silver frames.

"It'll be perfectly all right if we keep our heads," said Peter in his most dogmatic voice.

Lee looked round at him. It was rather an odd look.

"Oh, Peter dear," she said, and there was a pitying sound in the words. It was as if she was much older since the yesterdays when they used to quarrel. She felt old, and sad, and tolerant, and wise, and very sorry for Peter, because she couldn't see any way out of this without somebody being hurt, and she was afraid, not for herself, but for him.

Peter went on.

"Everything will be absolutely all right, only—Lee, you're not listening, and you've got to listen. They may send for one of us at any moment. They won't be so long over Peterson and Rush, and then it's pretty sure to be either you or me."

"I wonder whether Rush saw Mavis go out," said Lee quickly.

"That's just it. I hope he didn't. But whether he saw her or not, it's going to be very nearly impossible to keep Mavis out of this. You see, there were those two glasses, both used, and the very first thing the police will do is to find out where Ross spent the evening and who was with him. Well, he's always at the Ducks and Drakes. Everyone knows him there, and if she's been going out with him half as much as Lucy's been complaining about, it's ten to one that most of them will know Mavis, and the minute this show is in the papers they'll be tumbling over each other to tell the police that she was there with him last night. Unfortunately I was at the Ducks and Drakes myself, and if I'm asked I shall have to say that I saw Ross and Mavis there, because when dozens of other people must have seen them it will only add to the general fishiness if I pretend I didn't. What I do hope is that they won't have any proof that she came back here. I'll hold my tongue about that if no one else saw her. What about you?"

Lee drew in her breath.

"I shan't say anything either."

Peter squared his shoulders.

"I don't really give a damn about Mavis. She got herself into this, and we're all going to want a lot of luck to get her out of it. But it's you—" he came over to Lee and dropped his hands on her shoulders—"you, my dear—*you*. They'll ask you all sorts of questions. They may press you pretty hard. Because you don't belong here, and your coming in like that just on the very night that Ross was shot—well, it's bound to make them sit up and take notice."

Lee's eyelids lifted slowly and she looked up at him. She was not nearly so pretty as Mavis—the features too irregular, and just now her whole aspect too pale, too drawn with fatigue. But she had eyes which would be beautiful even when she was old. Something in the shape, something in the way that they were set, something in the shadow which the lashes cast—very dark lashes, thick, and dark, and fine—something in the deep, changing grey of the iris. Peter's heart always stirred in him when Lee looked up at him as she was looking now. But this time it stirred to a pulse of fear. His hand tightened on hers, and he said,

"You've got to hold your tongue about yourself, my dear. You came here, you were very tired, and you went to bed. You slept all night, and when you heard the commotion on the landing you came out to see what was going on. And that's all. Do you hear? That's *all*."

"Peter—"

He shook her a little.

"It's true, isn't it? You did go to bed and sleep all night, and that's all you know."

She kept her eyes on his face.

"Peter—" Her voice went away to just a breath. "Peter—weren't there any—footprints—inside that door?"

If he had thought there was the slightest chance of persuading her that the whole thing was a dream, and that there never had been any footprints, Peter might have grasped at this serviceable lie, but as he saw no chance of getting Lee to believe in it he let it go. He said,

"That's all right—I smudged them out."

"How? Oh, Peter!"

"Well, I was waiting for Peterson. I rather banked on his doing just what he did do, tearing off downstairs to get Rush and leaving the door open, so I was all ready with some damp paper. If there were footprints, I knew I shouldn't have time to get rid of them altogether, but I thought I could bank on being able to mess them up so that they couldn't possibly be identified. I'd plenty of time to do it, get back, get rid of the paper, wash my hands, and run out in my dressing-gown to join Peterson when he came back with Rush."

"It was very clever of you." Lee's lashes fell for a

moment and then rose again. "Peter, do you think I did it?" she said in an exhausted voice.

She startled him horribly. He said,

"What do you mean?" And then, on a quick note of anger, "Don't be a damned little fool!"

Lee stepped back from him, her gaze mournful and steady.

"No, Peter—please—I can't bear it. It's all shut up inside me, and if I can't talk about it—oh, don't you see?"

He saw, and the anger went out of him. He said,

"What do you want to talk about?"

"I want to tell you. I'm so afraid. It's no good just bottling it up, and I can't tell anyone else. You see, it was rather horrid about those Merville people. I don't know whether she ever meant to sail. I've begun to think perhaps she didn't. Anyhow at the last minute they had a row, and she walked out and took the child. I don't know if it was a real row. It may have been, because he was awfully worked up. And he didn't want to let me go—yes, I know—you said so all along, and we quarrelled about it. And you were perfectly right, which is lovely for you but not quite so much fun for me. But that doesn't matter now. What does matter is this. That Merville man was just slime—he really was. And when he took hold of me I saw scarlet, and, Peter, if I could have got my hands on a pistol I'd have shot him. I would, and I'd have liked doing it." The colour came into her face just for a moment and then ebbed again.

Peter controlled his voice to a careless tone.

"A good riddance, but possibly a bit awkward. On the whole, just as well that there wasn't a pistol."

Lee nodded.

"I know. And I got away all right. I threw the big inkstand at him and the ink went into his eyes. I didn't wait after that." There was a faint satisfaction in her tone, but the strained note came back again. "I got here, and I was most awfully tired, but I didn't feel like going to sleep. I rummaged round for a book, and I found a stupid murder story. It really was stupid, and I didn't get very far with it, because I went to sleep, and the last bit I remember was about a man creeping down a long passage in the dark, and when he'd got about half way he found a pistol, and all at once a door opened at the other end and he saw the most dreadful face looking at him, and he fired at it with the pistol he had just picked up. As if anyone *would!*''

"What has all this got to do with Ross?"

"It might have started me off dreaming. I did dream, you know, and I did walk in my sleep, and I did go into Ross's flat. If my footprints were there, it proves that I went in." Her voice dropped wretchedly. "If I could only remember what the dream was about. But suppose—just suppose I got that murder story all mixed up in a dream with René Merville. I might—have taken—Ross's pistol—and if he caught hold of me, I might have—thought he was René—and I might—have shot him—'' The last word scarcely sounded. She put out a hand to steady herself against the back of the chair.

Peter pushed his hands deep into his pockets where he could clench them unseen, and remarked,

"My child, you'll have to take to writing thrillers yourself. That's a marvellous effort of the imagination. But I don't think I should produce it for the Inspector. Nobody admires the police more than I do, but imagination just isn't their strong suit. They have an earthy preference for facts, you know—things like—"

"Footprints," said Lee.

CHAPTER
XIV

DETECTIVE ABBOTT USHERED in Mr. Peter Renshaw. He gave his name as Peter Craddock Renshaw, and admitted to eight years' service in the Westshire regiment, at present stationed at Lahore in Northern India. He was at home on leave, and was occupying the flat of his late cousin, Miss Mary Craddock, whose executor he was.

"Now, Mr. Renshaw," said the Inspector, "I believe you are Mr. Craddock's next of kin. Do you happen to know whether he made a will?"

Peter did a stupid thing. He said at once and without thinking,

"I'm pretty sure he didn't."

"And what makes you think that, Mr. Renshaw?"

He was in for it now. It would be the worst possible folly to hesitate.

"Well, it was something he said. I can't remember how it came up, but it was something to do with my being my cousin's executor—something on the lines of he hadn't made a will and he wasn't going to, because he didn't give a damn who had his money when he was gone."

"And there was a good deal of money?"

"Quite a piece," said Mr. Renshaw soberly.

The Inspector leaned forward.

"You're telling me Mr. Craddock was a wealthy man—and he lived in a little flat like this?"

"Yes, he did. But there were reasons. His father had a lot, but the depression hit them very hard indeed. My uncle had to economize, cut everything to the bone. He died about four years ago. But the reason I said there was quite a piece of money is that a lot of leasehold property fell in this year. I've no idea of the amount, but it was something pretty considerable."

"And if there's no will—you're next of kin and heir at law, I take it."

"I suppose I am—if there's no will." Peter went on looking at the Inspector for a moment, then he turned and looked at Detective Abbott.

Detective Abbott was looking at the ceiling. Something ran a sharp pin into Peter's memory and jogged it. He said to himself, "Fug Abbott, or I'm a Dutchman!" He very nearly said it aloud.

The Inspector's voice recalled him to the fact that he was undergoing an official examination, and that he had just said several things that could very easily be used against him.

"Mr. Craddock's solicitor has informed us that Mr. Craddock was very much opposed to the idea of making a will. As far as he knows, no will exists. Would you say that this was common knowledge in the family?"

"It might be."

"Other relatives might expect to benefit by Mr. Craddock's death if he died intestate?"

Peter didn't like the way that this was tending. He said quickly,

"I don't know, but some of the property is entailed. Didn't old Pettigrew tell you so?"

The Inspector did not answer this question.

"Entailed upon you, Mr. Renshaw?"

"I am quite sure Mr. Pettigrew must have told you that. It's all down in old David Craddock's will."

"You seem very well informed as to the provisions of this will."

Peter felt a certain anger, but he kept his voice quiet.

"I told you I was acting as executor to my old cousin. I have had to look up the provisions of my great-grandfather's will. There was some small trust, and there was a question as to whether her share went to her surviving sister, or whether it would have to be shared with a niece."

"The niece's name?"

"Mavis Grey."

"Seems to me, Mr. Renshaw, there's a lot of you in this—all relations. Now I'd like to get those relationships clear, if you don't mind."

Peter slewed round to the table.

"If I can have a bit of paper, I'll put them down for you."

He had his bit of paper and the scarlet pen offered him gravely by Detective Abbott. He wrote, drew lines, and handed the result to the Inspector.

"The Craddock family tree. We're all there, I think."

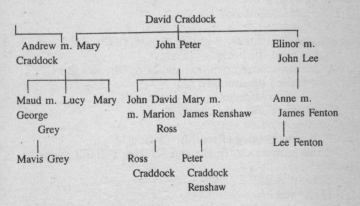

The Inspector studied it with a good deal of concentration.

"You and Mr. Craddock were first cousins then, and the young lady, Miss Fenton, a bit further afield. Mr. Craddock wasn't married, I take it."

"I never heard of a wife."

As Detective Abbott wrote this down, it occurred to him

to wonder whether there had been something that wasn't quite an emphasis on the last word.

"Well, now that we've got all that quite clear, Mr. Renshaw, may I trouble you for your account of what happened last night?"

"Certainly. I came home just before twelve o'clock—"

"Just a moment. You'd been dining out?"

"At the Luxe."

"And you spent the evening at the Luxe?"

"No—I went on to a night-club to meet some friends—a Mr. and Mrs. Nelson."

"I'd just like the name of the club."

"The Ducks and Drakes."

"Ah! Go on, Mr. Renshaw."

Peter went on.

"I got back here a little before twelve."

"That was rather early."

"It was very hot. The party broke up."

"No unpleasantness?"

"Certainly not."

"No unpleasantness with Mr. Craddock?"

"Look here, Inspector—"

"I'd like an answer to that question, Mr. Renshaw."

Peter smiled disarmingly.

"Well, the answer is in the negative."

"You didn't see your cousin?"

"Certainly I saw him."

"And where did you see Mr. Craddock?"

"I saw him at the Ducks and Drakes. I didn't speak to him."

"Sure of that?"

"Quite sure."

"Now why didn't you speak to him? Were you on bad terms?"

Peter shrugged his shoulders.

"I was with my party, and he was with his. We didn't meet, that's all."

"You didn't answer my question. I asked if you were on bad terms with him."

"Not bad, not good. We hadn't much in common, that's all."

"I see," said the Inspector. "Who was Mr. Craddock with?"

He had seen the question coming and known that he would be bound to answer it. Anyone at the Ducks and Drakes could put a name to Mavis. It would be fatal to hesitate. He said at once,

"Oh, he was with Miss Grey."

"Miss Grey—she was an intimate friend of Mr. Craddock's?"

Again it would not do to hang back.

"A cousin," he said carelessly.

"Miss Mavis Grey?"

"Miss Mavis Grey."

"Ah! Were Mr. Craddock and Miss Grey still at the Ducks and Drakes when you came away?"

"Yes, they were."

"Go on, Mr. Renshaw."

"I came home, I went to bed, and I went to sleep. I was roused by Peterson's yell. I got on my dressing-gown and came out on to the landing. I followed him and Rush into this room, and saw my cousin lying dead."

The Inspector leaned forward and raised his voice.

"And you picked up the revolver. I want to know what you did that for, Mr. Renshaw."

"I know," said Peter in a candid tone. "I oughtn't to have touched it. Rush ticked me off like anything."

The Inspector banged with his fist on the table.

"You took hold of it by the butt, and you took hold of it by the muzzle, and if there were fingermarks on either, you took very good care to destroy them—and I want to know why."

Peter gazed at him earnestly.

"Of course I knew the minute I'd done it that I ought to have left the damned thing alone."

The Inspector banged again.

"And I'm asking you why you didn't leave it alone."

Peter knitted his brows.

"Well, I suppose it was the shock. The first thing I knew I'd picked the thing up."

"And the next thing you knew you were handling it all over!"

"Well, it's no good going on ticking me off. I mean—well is it? I must have done a bit of—what do they call it—unconscious cerebration, or I wouldn't have done it, would I? I've apologized, and I don't quite see what more I can do. I mean, it's no good crying over spilt milk, is it, Inspector?"

"I should like to know why the milk was spilt," said Inspector Lamb in a most unpleasant tone of voice.

Peter nodded thoughtfully.

"You know," he said, "when there's an emergency you don't think, you just do things. Afterwards someone comes along and asks why you did them, just like you're doing now, and you haven't a single earthly notion. It's natural you should come over all suspicious, but don't you see, if I was a calculating criminal I should know exactly why I'd done everything, because I should have had it all mapped out, so that really, instead of getting suspicious because I can't give you even the most silly-ass explanation, you ought to regard it as a proof of my innocence."

The Inspector took a good hard look at him. Peter sustained the look.

He had to sustain the thrust of a sudden question.

"What time did you hear the shot?"

Without batting an eyelid he said,

"I didn't hear it."

The Inspector squared up to him.

"Now look here, Mr. Renshaw, I've seen your flat. That wall you're sitting with your back to at this minute is the wall of the bedroom in which you slept last night. Do you mean to tell me that you slept with your head right up against that wall and didn't hear the shot that killed your cousin?"

"I'm not telling you anything of the sort. You see, I didn't sleep in there last night. I went to bed there, but—well, it was a hot night and I thought I'd be cooler in the other room—the breeze was that way—so I slept on the sofa in the sitting-room.''

The Inspector looked him straight in the eye.

"Are you going to swear at the inquest that you didn't hear that shot?"

"Without a tremor. You see, it happens to be true. After all, you know, Inspector, there's quite a lot of traffic along here at night, and one gets used to it. There's not a lot to choose between a backfire and a revolver shot. My first night or two here I couldn't sleep. Now it's got me the other way round and I can't wake up.''

"And you didn't wake up last night? Are you going to swear that you didn't get up and go into your cousin's flat and quarrel with him?"

"I am."

"Well then, Mr. Renshaw, I think that will be all for the moment. Have you any objection to letting us take your fingerprints?''

Peter smiled broadly.

"Oh, no objection at all. But you've got them already, haven't you? The—er—weapon must have been fairly well plastered.''

CHAPTER

XV

P ETER WALKED UP and down in Lucy Craddock's sitting-room and waited for Lee to come back.

They didn't keep her long, but they kept her long enough for a young man in a state of strain to have several kinds of nightmares about what they might be asking her behind those two closed doors and what she might be answering. When she did come he thought she looked relieved.

"What did they ask you?"

"Not very much." She sat down in the biggest chair and leaned back. Her brief white linen dress left her arms bare right up to the shoulder. She stretched them out on the big padded arms of the chair and closed her eyes.

"What do you mean by not very much?"

The soft lashes lay on her cheek.

"Just what you said. They wanted to know when I got here, and when I went to bed, and when I got up, and whether I heard the shot."

"You didn't."

"I told them I didn't. They asked me whether I was friends with Ross."

"What did you say to that?"

The lashes flickered.

"I said not particularly. And then they asked about

Mavis—whether she was a friend of mine, whether she was a friend of yours, and whether she was a friend of Ross's.''

"And you said?''

"That she wasn't particularly my friend or yours, but that she and Ross were friendly. It wasn't any good my saying they weren't, because Miss Bingham would be quite sure to give that away. She was going in as I came out.'' Lee's eyes opened suddenly and wide. "Oh, Peter—do you suppose she heard anything? It's a frightful thought!''

"We can't do anything about it if she did,'' said Peter gloomily.

He came and sat down on the floor in front of the big chair and laid his cheek against her hand.

"Don't let's bother about all these beastly people. Are you glad you didn't go to South America?''

The hand just moved against his cheek.

"I don't know—there wouldn't be any policemen—''

"If you were in South America with that dago you might be very glad to see a policeman.''

She tried to pull away her hand, but he caught it just in time. He began to kiss the palm.

"You want someone to look after you, my girl—that's what you do.''

Just at the moment it sounded rather nice. She sighed, and Peter said,

"I'm going to marry you out of hand, you know.''

The lashes were down again. There was more colour in the cheek on which they rested.

"Are you?''

"I think it can be done in about three days.''

"Don't I have anything to say about it?'' She spoke in a soft, sleepy voice.

"Not very much. You can be there if you're good.''

"Thank you, darling.''

Peter kneeled up and took her in his arms.

"Lee, you will—you *will*—you really will.''

Her eyes opened. They looked startlingly dark and clear. They met his own, and without a word denied him.

"Lee—''

It was a long time before she said "No."

"Why?" said Peter in an angry voice.

Something sparkled behind the fallen lashes.

"You can't marry everyone who asks you."

"I don't want you to. I want you to marry me."

"I can't think why."

"You're not required to think—you're not very good at it anyhow."

She opened her eyes and sat up.

"Peter, what an odious husband you'd make!"

"No, I shouldn't. I should make a very good husband indeed. I have all the qualities you require—good thinking-apparatus, reliable character, honest, sober, hard-working—"

"What Nanna used to call a good-living young man," said Lee, still with the sparkle.

"Well, you do know the worst of me."

"We should quarrel."

"Of course. All happily married couples quarrel."

A light shiver went over her.

"What's the matter?"

"Peter—when you said that—it sounded so nice and ordinary. Do you think we shall ever get back to being nice and ordinary again?"

"I hope so," said Peter.

CHAPTER
XVI

M ISS BINGHAM CAME in with little tripping steps. Her head was poked forward and her eyes went here, there and everywhere. They had taken up the rug in the hall and washed the parquet. Such a relief. And in here, where poor Mr. Craddock's body had lain in that shocking pool of blood—yes, that rug was gone too. And the parquet did really cover the whole of the floor. She had always wondered about that, because it might have been just a surround, and Lucy Craddock, who ought to have known, never seemed to be sure about it or take any interest. Even in her cradle Miss Bingham had always taken an interest in everything.

She sat and preened herself in the chair which Detective Abbott set for her. She had dressed as carefully as if she were going to a wedding or a bazaar, the two most exciting social events within her orbit. But this was far more exciting than either. Everyone went to bazaars and weddings, but to be an important witness in a sensational murder case was something to distinguish one for ever.

She wore her best dress, a brown artificial silk with rather a bright zigzag orange pattern, and she had put on a new hair-net. She was very proud of the fact that there was so little grey in her hair. There wasn't very much of it, but back-combed and well fluffed up under the net it could be made the best of, and it was still a very good dark brown. Under the fuzzy fringe and the rather marked dark eyebrows, Miss Bingham's eyes were as sharp and bright and restless as a squirrel's, and her cheeks as hard and red as August apples. There were a great many inquisitive lines about the eyes, and two very heavy ones running down from the nose to the chin. It was these lines which gave the upper lip a rather jutting appearance. About her neck Miss Bingham wore a long gold chain which had been her father's watchchain, and a string of bog-oak beads which had belonged to her mother.

She sat on the edge of her chair, and gave her name as Wilhelmina Ethel Bingham, unmarried. She occupied flat No. 12, immediately over Miss Mary Craddock's flat.

"That is to say, Inspector, it *was* Miss Mary Craddock's flat. A very dear friend of mine—a very dear friend indeed, and a most patient sufferer. An example to us all, I'm sure—"

"Quite so," said the Inspector. "Mr. Renshaw is now occupying the flat."

Miss Bingham bridled.

"I could hardly fail to be aware of *that*. All the years I have lived above Miss Craddock I never had to complain about a sound, but from the time Mr. Renshaw came in it has been a very different story."

"Noisy—eh?" said the Inspector.

Miss Bingham slightly closed her eyes.

"Would you believe me if I were to tell you that he throws his boots across the room, positively *throws* them, every night when he takes them off—*and* several times during the day."

"Very disturbing," said the Inspector. "Well now, Miss Bingham, I can see you're a lady that notices things. What I want to know is whether you noticed anything unusual last night."

"Indeed I did, Inspector—and I can only say that, shocking as it all is, I am not surprised. Over and over again I have said both to Lucy and to Mary Craddock that what was going on in this house was a scandal—right under their noses too. Over and over again I've said that something would happen if it went on. Why, I've even thought of moving—after being here ten years—so that will show you how I've felt about it."

The Inspector cleared his throat.

"About last night, Miss Bingham—"

"Yes, yes—oh, yes. But we must take everything in order, mustn't we, Inspector?" She rummaged in a black suede bag and produced a rather crumpled sheet of paper. "Method—that's what I always say. Most important, isn't it? I am sure you will agree. I have made a few jottings—just a few heads, you know—and if you will permit me, I will keep to my heads. 'Begin at the beginning and keep straight on to the end.' That is what my dear father used to say, and I have found it a most excellent rule." She coughed slightly. "My first head—"

The Inspector pushed his chair back with a loud scraping sound.

"I should be obliged if you would keep to the point, Miss Bingham."

"Yes, yes—so very necessary—I quite agree."

"Since you have been here so long and are acquainted with all these people—"

"Yes, yes—that brings me to my first head—Mr. Craddock's Relations with his Relations—a humorous touch which I could hardly resist, though perhaps in the circumstances not quite suitable."

Inspector Lamb drew a long breath.

"I shall be glad to hear anything you have to say on that subject."

He received an arch glance.

"Method, you see, Inspector—method. That was my first head. It is, naturally, painful to me to have to say so, but I feel I must be perfectly frank, and I can only say that Mr. Craddock's relations with his—er—relatives were not at all good. Oh, dear me, no—quite the reverse. My poor friend Lucy Craddock cried to me, positively cried, over his dissipated ways and his total lack of consideration for the family name and for her feelings. I happen to know that she was most distressed and anxious over his scandalous pursuit of her niece.''

"Was that Miss Mavis Grey?''

"Yes, Mavis Grey. I see you have already heard something on that point. Over and over again Lucy begged him to desist. And only yesterday I happened to be coming down the stairs, and I saw him pushing my poor friend, actually pushing her, out of his front door, and I heard what he said. Anyone might have heard it, for he spoke quite loud—and how a man who had had the upbringing of a gentleman could so far forget himself—''

"What did he say?''

Miss Bingham tossed her head.

"'Old maid cousins should be seen and not heard.' That's what he said! And poor Lucy stood there just as if she had been turned to stone, until Peter Renshaw came upstairs, and when he asked her what was the matter she burst out crying and said, 'He's wicked!' And I know, because Mrs. Green told me, that he was going to turn Lucy out! After she'd been thirty years in that flat of hers! I don't wonder she said he was wicked!''

"Mr. Craddock's relations with Miss Lucy Craddock were not good then. Now what about Mr. Renshaw? What sort of terms was he on with him?''

"Not at all good terms,'' said Miss Bingham, shaking her head. "Why, I've seen Mr. Renshaw walk all the way up the stairs rather than go in the lift with his cousin. Oh, yes, anyone could tell you that they didn't get on—oh, no, not at all.''

"And Miss Fenton?''

"Well, I couldn't say very much about Miss Fenton. She's not a young woman I care for particularly—far too off-hand in her manner. I believe Lucy Craddock is very fond of her. I can't think why, because the girl quite refused to be guided by Lucy's advice and insisted, absolutely insisted, on going off to South America or somewhere. I may say I was most surprised to find that she was here in Lucy Craddock's flat. I quite understood that she had started for South America.''

"You didn't know of any ill feeling between her and Mr. Craddock?"

A disappointed look crossed Miss Bingham's face. She did the best she could.

"They were not at all friendly," she said. "And that brings me to my second head—Events of Last Night."

The Inspector hitched himself up in his chair. Detective Abbott, who had been gazing at the ceiling, brought his eyes to the writing-table again. Eavesdropping old cats had their uses. She might have something to tell, or she might not. He thought she had. She looked like a cat who had been at the cream, and—oh gosh, what a witness she was going to make!

She was speaking.

"Of course, I don't know, Inspector, what Mr. Renshaw has told you. I have had no communication with him, I can assure you. He may have made a frank and honest statement, or he may not—it is not for me to say. I am making no allegations. If I have my suspicions, it is because my knowledge of human nature tells me that young men are very unreliable when there is a young woman in the case. Even Lucy Craddock, who has been regrettably weak with her, is forced to admit that the girl is a flirt. Though why anyone should think her pretty I do *not* understand, but a young man like Peter Renshaw—"

The Inspector leaned forward and raised his voice.

"Here, Miss Bingham, what are you talking about?"

Miss Bingham opened her black suede bag, rummaged in it, said "Dear, dear!" under her breath, rummaged again, produced a clean folded pocket handkerchief with a mauve border, dabbed at her nose to remove a bead of moisture from its tip, and said sharply,

"Mavis Grey and Peter Renshaw."

"What about them?"

She threw him a bright, triumphant look.

"Then he didn't tell you."

"He didn't tell me what?"

"That she spent the night in his flat."

The Inspector hit the writing-table with the palm of his left hand.

"Who spent the night in whose flat?"

Miss Bingham coughed.

"Of course you realize, Inspector, that this is an awkward subject. It is, naturally, very unpleasant for me to have to mention such a thing, but when it comes to murder—"

"Who spent the night in whose flat?" said Inspector Lamb.

Miss Bingham shook her head.

"I felt sure he wouldn't tell you. Such a false code of honour. Very wrong—very wrong indeed. Perhaps I had better tell you what I saw and heard."

"I think you had."

Miss Bingham glanced at her crumpled sheet of paper.

"I had been beginning at the beginning. Method, you know, method. I have a portable wireless set—with earphones, because I do *not* think it right to disturb others for my own pleasure. Most inconsiderate—most inconsiderate and selfish, is what I always have said and always will say. So I use earphones."

Detective Abbott looked at the ceiling. How much of this could old Lamb stand before he started to foam and bite the carpet?

Miss Bingham patted her hair-net complacently and continued.

"I take the second news, and after that I retire for the night. I do not generally put my light out until half past eleven. I may have been a little later than that last night, but it would not be more than a few minutes. I did not go to sleep. I heard Mr. Renshaw come in. My clock struck twelve just about then, and it was no use my thinking about sleep until he had finished going to bed. He has a peculiarly noisy way of opening and shutting drawers. Really, after having my dear friend Mary Craddock there for so long it is most disturbing, most unpleasantly disturbing. Then when I did get to sleep, it seemed to me that I was almost immediately awakened. It was a sound that had waked me, I am sure—something of an unusual nature."

"Was it a shot?"

"That is what I cannot say. My bedroom is over the sitting-room of Mary Craddock's flat. She used the larger and better room as a bedroom on account of being an invalid, so I was not so near to Mr. Craddock's flat as if I had been in my sitting-room, but I had all the doors open inside the flat. The night was exceptionally sultry, and I am convinced that the sound I heard came from the floor below, and from the direction of number eight. I am sure of this, because my first thought was that Mr. Craddock had no business to disturb us all in the middle of the night. I put on my dressing-gown and went out on the landing. The light burns there all night, but I turned it out because I naturally did not wish to be seen. I then went a little way down the stairs and looked over the banisters. Oh, Inspector—what did I see?"

"You'd better tell us," said the Inspector drily.

Miss Bingham's eyes were glittering with excitement.

"Well, there was Mr. Craddock in his doorway with his hand up to his head and blood all over it. And there was Peter Renshaw over by his door, and that girl Mavis Grey with her arms round his neck, crying, and sobbing, and saying, 'Oh, don't let him touch me!'"

"You say you saw all this. Where were you?"

"Of course I saw it all! You don't think I would make a thing like that up, I hope! I looked between the banisters, and through the lift shaft. There is only the steel framework when the lift isn't up. And Mr. Renshaw said, 'What have you done to her?' And Mr. Craddock said he hadn't done anything. And he said it was the girl who had hurt him—at least that is what he meant."

"What did he *say?*"

"He said, 'I was the one that got hurt.' And he said, 'I've had enough.' And then Mr. Renshaw took that girl into poor Mary Craddock's flat and banged the door."

"Is that all you heard them say? Remember that this is important and you must be as accurate as you can. Don't leave anything out, and don't put anything in."

"You needn't caution me about being accurate, Inspector.

Often and often my friends have told me that I have an absolutely photographic memory. Now let me see—he said that girl had hurt him—"

"I don't think that is quite accurate."

"That is what he meant," said Miss Bingham firmly. "He looked quite dazed, and I'm sure the blood was simply pouring down his face. And I've always said that if a girl leads a man on she has only herself to thank for what happens. What was she doing in his flat at one o'clock in the morning? Shameless, I call it—shameless! And then she throws her arms round Peter Renshaw's neck and says, 'Don't let him touch me!' "

"In fact, you gathered that Mr. Craddock had alarmed Miss Grey to such an extent that she threw herself on Mr. Renshaw's protection after striking Mr. Craddock with— well, there's no harm in saying that it must have been the decanter, because we found it broken and there was glass in the wound."

"But that wouldn't have killed him, Inspector."

"Mr. Craddock was shot." The Inspector's tone was curt. "Now, Miss Bingham, I should like to know how Miss Grey was dressed, if you don't mind."

"Full evening dress, Inspector. Silver *lamé,* and her poor Aunt Mary not dead a month! I don't know what girls are coming to! And no back to it!"

The Inspector wiped his brow.

"Well, what happened after Mr. Renshaw and Miss Grey had gone into number nine?"

"Mr. Craddock went back into his flat."

"And then?"

Miss Bingham hesitated, sniffed slightly, and said,

"I wanted to see if that shameless girl was really going to stay."

"How long did you wait?"

"Half an hour. I said to myself, 'I will give her half an hour, and if she doesn't come out then, well, I shall know what to think.' And I *did.* It was exactly half past one when I put my light out."

"That puts the murder at some time after half past one. After you put your light out did you go to sleep?"

"Not immediately—oh, no, I was too much horrified and disgusted. I heard the clock strike two."

"And no sound from down below?"

"Not then."

"What do you meant by not then?"

"Ah!" Miss Bingham put up a hand and pulled at her bog-oak necklace. "Ah! That is where I feel that my evidence is extremely important, because if Mr. Craddock was shot, you must of course want to know when the shot was fired."

"Did you hear it?" said the Inspector quickly.

Miss Bingham looked at him archly.

"I heard something. But I mustn't say it was a shot, must I—not unless I am perfectly sure, because of course I shall be on my oath, and you said yourself that I must be very accurate."

Inspector Lamb controlled himself and sat back.

"Would you kindly tell me what you heard, Miss Bingham?"

"Ah, but that is just what I cannot do, Inspector. I woke up—I am an extremely light sleeper, and there was something very heavy passing down the road. The traffic is shocking nowadays—so bad for the nervous system."

The Inspector's voice grated a little as he said,

"I am not asking you about the traffic. I am asking you if you heard anything that might have been a shot."

Miss Bingham shook a finger at him reprovingly.

"Ah, yes, yes—but don't you see that if the shot was fired at that moment, it is very unlikely that anyone would have heard it. The vehicle that was passing must have been exceptionally heavy—one of those great brewer's drays perhaps. And—it is extremely shocking to think of—but would not a person who meant to make a murderous attack on Mr. Craddock be likely to avail himself of just such an opportunity? I can assure you that the windows quite rattled."

"To say that a thing might happen isn't to say that it did

happen," said the Inspector tersely. "I'm afraid if that is all you have to tell us—"

"Oh, but it isn't!" said Miss Bingham. "Oh, no—not by any means. I don't know whether I went to sleep again or not—you see what an accurate witness I am—I may have done, or I may not. I am inclined to think I did, because I have a vague recollection of a dream in which I was skiing with the dear Vicar. Not that either of us has ever done so, but one sees pictures, and of course dreams are so very absurd, are they not? Well, well, I mustn't digress, but, you see, I must really have dropped off, perhaps just for a minute, perhaps for longer, and then I woke up again. I don't know if you are at all psychic, Inspector—"

The Inspector said "Certainly not!" in a barking tone. Detective Abbott covered his mouth with his hand.

"All the Binghams are psychic," said Miss Bingham with pride. "My grandfather—but no, I merely want you to understand how it was that I awaked in a state of great uneasiness. The atmosphere was most menacing. I felt an immediate necessity to investigate. I put on the light and looked at the clock. It was five minutes to three. I slipped on my dressing-gown and opened my front door. I was immediately struck by the fact that no light came up from below. As I told you before, I had put out the light on my own landing at a little before one, but it is usual for these lights to remain on all night. I could see by looking down the lift shaft that none of the landings were lit. There was a faint light in the hall, but all the landings were dark. This meant that the lights had been turned out by someone for reasons best known to himself. I went down to the turn of the stair, and as I stood there listening I distinctly heard someone move. I heard a door shut, and I heard someone move. And then, just as my eyes were getting accustomed to the darkness, the door of poor Mary Craddock's flat was opened and the light went on in her hall, and there was that girl Mavis Grey coming in from the landing with her dress clutched up in her hand where it was torn, and there was Peter Renshaw in the hall. And they shut the door and I didn't see anything more."

The Inspector jerked forward.

"Miss Grey was going into the flat? You're sure of that?"

"I am quite sure, Inspector."

"And Mr. Renshaw—was he going in too?"

Miss Bingham hesitated.

"I don't know. He might have been. He was in the hall."

Detective Abbott spoke for the first time. He said in an undertone,

"If they had both been out of the flat, he wouldn't pass her and go in first—I beg your pardon, sir."

The Inspector nodded.

"No—that's right. Miss Bingham, you say Miss Grey's dress was torn. Was it torn when you saw her at one o'clock?"

Miss Bingham primmed her mouth.

"It was disgracefully torn—I noticed it at once—she was quite dishevelled."

"The first time?"

"Oh, yes—at one o'clock. I noticed it at once."

The Inspector got thankfully to his feet.

"Thank you, Miss Bingham, that will do."

CHAPTER
XVII

THE INSPECTOR LOOKED at his watch. If Miss Mavis Grey was at home she ought to be here within the next quarter of an hour.

"Good job I'd told Lintott to fetch her along as soon as Mr. Renshaw let on that it was her with Mr. Craddock at the Ducks and Drakes last night. Looks as if she might have quite a piece to tell us if that Miss Bingham wasn't making her story up."

"I don't think she was making it up," said Detective Abbott.

"There's no saying what a spiteful woman will make up. And when you know as much about 'em as I do, my lad, you'll know that the only thing you can be sure of about any of 'em, good or bad, is that you never can be sure about anything. They try and fox you, and then if you catch 'em out, they up and laugh and say they weren't trying, and the next thing you know they're at it again. Here, ring up Mr. Grey's house, and if Lintott's still there, you tell him to ask Miss Grey for the silver dress she was wearing last night, and tell him to bring it along. I want to have a look at it, see? There's the address and the telephone number on the paper we got from Rush. And when you've done that I think I'll just have a word with Mr. Peter Renshaw."

Detective Abbott busied himself with the telephone. He

caught Lintott, delivered his message, and went to collect Peter. He found him in Miss Lucy Craddock's flat, and had a glimpse through the open sitting-room door of Miss Lee Fenton, all eyes and very pale. Peter, who had opened the front door, said,

"Hullo—again?" And then, "I say, you are Fug Abbott, aren't you?"

"Off duty," said Detective Abbott suavely. "At the moment—"

"You're a myrmidon of the law. Well, well—any use asking you to drop in when you are off duty—or is the position too delicate?"

"I don't know. Of course, anything you said—"

"Would be used against me. Well, put it to the Inspector if you like, and come if you can. We needn't talk murders." He smiled an odd, twisted smile. "You know where to find me."

They came back into Ross Craddock's flat. The Inspector was looking out of the window. Peter took up a position in front of the fireplace with his hands in his pockets. He had had enough of the chair—the prisoner was accommodated with a chair—no, thank you!

Inspector Lamb came back from the window.

"Won't you sit down, Mr. Renshaw?"

"No, thank you, Inspector."

Detective Abbott sat to his notes again. The Inspector turned a frowning face and said,

"Mr. Renshaw, I have just taken a statement from Miss Bingham. She informs me that she saw Miss Mavis Grey enter your flat just before one A.M. last night, and again at five minutes to three. What have you to say about that?"

Well, what had he to say? If the old cat had actually seen Mavis, there wasn't very much to be said. They were bound to interrogate Mavis, and the only thing for Mavis to do was to tell the exact truth. But would she? He felt a considerable amount of doubt. And if she didn't stick to the truth, then anything he said was going to make things worse. In fact, least said, soonest mended.

He looked frankly at the Inspector.

"I don't think I've got anything to say."

"Mr. Renshaw, this is a very grave matter. You made a statement just now—"

"I made a statement which concerned myself and my own movements during the night. That statement was perfectly true."

"All of it, Mr. Renshaw—including your reason for sleeping on the sofa in the sitting-room? Do you still say that it was because the breeze was that side, or will you modify that and admit that you had given up your bedroom to Miss Grey?"

Peter smiled affably.

"It sounds better that way—on Miss Bingham's statement. That is to say, I'm not really admitting anything, you know, and if you want to heckle me about the breeze, I daresay I could prove that it was on that side of the house. As to Miss Grey's movements, I suggest that you ask her, not me. She's in a much better position to know what she was doing last night than I am." He smiled again in the pleasantest manner in the world. "You can't insist on my making a statement—can you?"

The Inspector did not smile. He said stiffly,

"All these statements are entirely voluntary. But at the same time I would like to point out—"

"That any failure to make one, or to do all in my power to assist the police would be highly suspicious. But you see, Inspector, I am doing my very best to assist you. I am suggesting that you apply to Miss Grey. She will probably tell you a great deal more than you want to know. Girls are like that." He cocked an eyebrow. "Miss Bingham, for instance. But of course that's all in the day's work."

The Inspector took no notice. He continued to frown, and said in an official voice,

"I would like your permission to search the flat you are occupying."

"My permission, Inspector? Why this formality?"

"Because I haven't got a search-warrant, and your permission will save time. Have you any objection to giving it?"

"Oh, none—none at all."

"Then when Lintott arrives you will perhaps accompany him. You had better be present."

"Just to see that he doesn't manufacture fingerprints and fabricate bloodstains? I see."

"Meanwhile—"

Peter laughed.

"Meanwhile, you'd like to keep me under your eye. All right, I don't mind. I've spent the last fortnight destroying things in that flat, and I'm fed up with it."

CHAPTER
XVIII

THE INSPECTOR WATCHED Miss Mavis Grey come into the room. Pretty girl—fine eyes—a lot of hair—plenty of paint on. Difficult to stop girls doing it nowadays, but if he found one of his with her mouth made up to look like orange peel he was going to have something to say about it. He kept his direct look on her, and saw her eyes widen and startle, and saw the colour in her cheeks go suddenly hard, as colour does when the skin beneath it blanches. She looked every way at once like a frightened horse, but the first place she looked at was the floor—just that space from which the rug had been rolled up and taken away.

Having seen these things, Inspector Lamb said good afternoon and invited her to sit down. He thought she was glad to reach the proffered chair. When she was seated he went out into the hall where Constable Lintott was waiting, shutting the door behind him. Mr. Peter Renshaw, who had been asked to wait in Mr. Craddock's bedroom, was summoned, and he and Lintott went over together to No. 9.

As soon as the door had closed behind the Inspector, Mavis Grey leaned back and relaxed. Perhaps he wasn't going to come back. Perhaps she would only have to talk to the young policeman who was writing at Ross's table. *Ross's table....* A giddy feeling came over her. She mustn't think about Ross. . . . It passed. She looked out under her eyelashes at the young policeman. It would be so much easier to talk to him than to that fat, red-faced man who had stared so hard when she came into the room. She hoped earnestly that he wasn't coming back. But as the thought went through her mind the door opened. He came in and sat down in the chair that was opposite hers. Much too near. She did hate people sitting as near to her as that— unless she liked them very much. She slid her chair back a few inches, and the Inspector said,

"When did you hear of Mr. Ross Craddock's death?"

All the things that they might possibly ask her had been going round, and round, and round in her head, but this was one which she had never thought of at all. She didn't know what to say. Her eyes filled with tears.

"The policeman—"

"You knew nothing about it until the constable informed you?"

She shook her head.

"And my uncle and aunt are out for the day. It's dreadful!"

"Murder commonly is," said the Inspector. "Now, Miss Grey, I have to ask you some questions. You are not on oath now, but you will be called as a witness at the inquest, and your evidence there will be given on your oath, so will you be as accurate as possible in your answers? Detective Abbott will take then down, and they will be read over to you afterwards. There's no need for you to be alarmed, but I hope you will tell us just what happened last night."

Mavis looked down at the grey and white muslin of her dress and the long white gloves she was holding. It was too hot to wear gloves. But her hands were not hot, they were deathly cold and damp.

She said, "Oh, yes," in a fluttering voice.

"You were at the Ducks and Drakes with Mr. Craddock?"

"Yes."

"What time did you leave?"

"I don't know."

"Would it be somewhere before one o'clock?"

"I think so. . . . Oh, yes, it was, because my uncle and

aunt really don't like my being out late—not just in the ordinary way, you know. I haven't got a key. They're very strict and old-fashioned, so it means that someone has to sit up.''

This was one of the bits she had thought about. She felt pleased with herself, because really she was doing it very well. She went on, hurrying to get it over.

"So when I knew how late I was going to be, I rang up and said I would spend the night with Isabel Young—that is, Mrs. James Young, Upton Villa, Carrisbroke Road, Hampstead, Garden City.''

"Hm!'' said the Inspector to himself, "Very pat with that address, aren't you?'' Then aloud, "And then you came back here with Mr. Craddock?''

Mavis's hands tightened on the gloves.

"Oh, no—of course I didn't. I went to Isabel's.''

He leaned forward.

"Miss Grey, I'm going to ask you to be careful. This is a murder case. Your friend Mrs. Young might say that you had stayed the night with her to get you out of a scrape with your uncle and aunt, but do you think she'll stand up and swear to it on her oath in a court of justice?''

Mavis looked at him in a perfectly terrified manner.

"I did go there.''

"Not at one o'clock, Miss Grey. You came back here with Mr. Craddock. You were seen here.''

Mavis said, "Oh!'' and lost her head. "Oh, I wasn't—who saw me? There wasn't anyone—Peter wouldn't—''

"It was not Mr. Peter Renshaw. He has referred me to you. Now, Miss Grey—you were seen, and the best thing you can do is to tell the truth. Lies won't get you anywhere, and trying to cover things up won't get you anywhere. You can't cover things up in a murder case.''

She leaned back, panting a little.

"It's all very stupid. Of course I'll tell you the truth. I really did mean to go to Isabel's. But it's such a long way, and when he—when Ross suggested that I should come back here and ask my cousin Lucy Craddock to put me up I thought I would.''

"Were you not aware that Miss Craddock was leaving for the Continent yesterday?"

"Ross said she had put off going—he really did, or I wouldn't have come back here with him—I really wouldn't. And when I found she *had* gone I just came in here to have a drink. And Ross was rude to me, so I went over to Peter, and he took me in."

The Inspector considered this a very economical description. It took him a good deal of questioning to fill in the details—the crash that had waked Miss Bingham, and probably Mr. Peter Renshaw as well; the decanter that had smashed over Mr. Craddock's head—and he seemed to have asked for it proper; and the girl's headlong flight, clutching her torn dress—well, that fitted in all right with what Miss Bingham had seen. She hadn't made any bones about it either, not once he got her going. He was left with no doubt in his mind that one cousin had been rude to her, and the other cousin had taken her in, and that except for a cut over the eye which he had richly deserved Mr. Ross Craddock was alive and hearty at 1 A.M. The question was, what had happened after that? Had Mr. Renshaw gone across to his cousin's flat and come to such terms with him over the girl that it had ended in a revolver shot? It might have happened that way. Words running high. One at least of the two men flushed with liquor. Mr. Craddock getting out his revolver perhaps, and having it snatched from him. Some sort of a struggle, and—the shot. And the girl running in on them. Yes, it might have been that way very easily. Against it only Abbott's remark—and by rights Abbott shouldn't be making remarks—that if he and Miss Grey had both been out of the flat, Mr. Renshaw wouldn't pass her and go in first."

He studied Miss Mavis Grey with his chin in his hand. He thought she looked like a girl who has said her piece and got it over. She had let go of those gloves she had been wringing into knots and was sitting back. Colour a bit more natural too. He said,

"Did you notice what time the shot was fired?" and saw her flinch.

She caught her breath and said all in a hurry,

"Oh, no—how could I? I never heard any shot."

"Not with your head right up against this wall? Mr. Renshaw gave you his bedroom, didn't he? I've had a look at the flat, and the head of the bed is not three yards from where you're sitting now, and not four from the place where Mr. Craddock was found. Come, come, Miss Grey, I think you must have heard that shot."

"Oh, but I didn't. I was so tired. I'd been dancing—it was so hot—I was dreadfully tired—I just slept. When I'm like that nothing wakes me—and there was a lot of traffic."

"Did you hear the traffic in your sleep? Be careful, Miss Grey. You say you were asleep. Did you undress?"

"I took my dress off."

"Then you must have put it on again, because you were wearing it when Miss Bingham saw you go back into Mr. Renshaw's flat at three o'clock in the morning."

"She couldn't—she didn't—I was asleep."

"She is prepared to swear that she did. Don't you think you had better tell me the truth, Miss Grey?"

A bright angry glow suffused the artificial colour in her cheeks and overflowed it. She clenched her hands over the gloves and said stubbornly,

"She saw me at one o'clock. She couldn't have seen me at three—I was in bed and asleep."

"Are you going to swear to that at the inquest?"

She gave a sort of gasp and said "Yes."

He went on looking at her hard for a moment, and then said in an easy conversational voice,

"What about that dress you were wearing last night? I'd like to have a look at it. Did Lintott bring it along?"

"I haven't got it. It was torn. I've thrown it away."

"Where?" said Inspector Lamb.

Mavis stared at him.

"Did you put it in your waste-paper basket, or what? If you did, I'm afraid Lintott will have to collect it, even if it's gone into the dustbin."

Mavis rushed into speech.

"I burnt it."

"Where did you burn it?"

"In my bedroom fire. It wasn't any use—it was all torn—I couldn't have worn it. I—''

"Do you generally have a fire in your bedroom when the temperature is over eighty? Come, come, Miss Grey, what have you done with that dress?''

There was a knock on the door. He looked over his shoulder and said "Come in."

Constable Lintott came into the room with a rolled-up bundle in his hand.

Mavis said "Oh!" and the Inspector said,

"Where did you find it, Lintott?"

"Chest of drawers in the bedroom—bottom drawer—pushed down under a lot of the old lady's things."

"All right, that'll do. Put it down."

Constable Lintott withdrew.

The Inspector got up out of his chair and shook out the bundle, which resolved itself into a long silver dress, a good deal torn, a good deal crushed. A large circular piece had been cut out of the front. He looked at Mavis, and Mavis looked at the dress. She hadn't cut away quite enough. The stain had spread. As that dreadful fat man stood there holding it up, anybody—*anybody* could see why the piece had been cut out. It had been cut out because it had been soaked in blood.

Mavis burst into tears. The Inspector's voice came to her through the sound of her own sobs.

"Now, Miss Grey—here's your own dress telling its story plain enough. You were in this flat after Mr. Craddock was shot. Perhaps you were here when the shot was fired. You were here, and you knelt down and got the front of your dress all messed up with his blood, and then you went back to number nine and Miss Bingham saw you. She saw Mr. Renshaw inside his own flat, and she saw you go in. Now you just come across with what you know. Was it Mr. Renshaw who fired that shot?"

"No, no—he didn't—oh, he didn't! Miss Bingham didn't see me. She's making it all up. She's a wicked old woman. I never came back. I tell you she couldn't have seen me—I was asleep."

The Inspector dropped the torn dress and came back to his chair.

"Pity to go on saying that sort of thing," he said, "but if that's what you want in your statement you can have it there. What were your relations with Mr. Craddock?"

The bright angry flush came up again. She stopped crying, and said,

"I don't know what you mean."

"I think you do. Was he your lover? Was he courting you? Had he asked you to marry him? Were you engaged to him?"

"Of course I wasn't! He liked me. He was a cousin, and we went about together, but there wasn't anything in it. I'm not engaged to anyone, but if I were—"

"If you were?"

Mavis hesitated, but only for a moment. It couldn't do any harm, and if it convinced them what nonsense it was to say this sort of thing about her and Ross, it might do quite a lot of good. She said in a defiant voice which still sounded tearful,

"If it were anyone, it would be Bobby Foster. He—he wants to, and I haven't exactly said I would, but—oh, well, it would be him if it was anyone."

"I see," said the Inspector.

CHAPTER
XIX

MAVIS GREY was shown out. Detective Abbott stood behind her in the hall of the flat and watched to see what she would do. She had had a fright and a shaking, and he thought she would want to talk to Peter Renshaw. Short of arresting her or him, or detaining either or both of them on suspicion, you couldn't prevent them talking things over, but of course it meant that she would tell him just what she had said and just what she hadn't said, and then he would have to go all out and back her up. Detective Abbott's opinion of Miss Mavis Grey was that she would say anything, without worrying about whether it was true or not, as long as she thought it would get her out of a mess.

She stood there for a moment, and then she went over to the door of No. 9 and rang the bell. Constable Lintott opened the door, a pleasant-looking young man with a rosy face and round blue eyes. Miss Grey was a good deal taken aback. She had had enough of policemen for the moment, and she wanted to see Peter. She said so in the rather haughty voice which very often means that a girl is afraid she is going to cry.

Constable Lintott directed her to No. 7, and put her in a dilemma. She wanted to see Peter, but she didn't want to see Lee Fenton. She wanted to get away from all these policemen, and she simply had to tidy up her face before she went out on the street. Her eyelids pricked, her skin felt sticky, and she was quite convinced that the tip of her nose was red. She crossed the landing again and rang the bell of No. 7.

It was Lee who opened the door, and as soon as Mavis saw her a wave of faintness came over her again. There was a mist, and a picture in the mist. But this time she made an effort, because she didn't want to faint, she wanted to talk to Peter. She walked past Lee into the sitting-room, and Peter looked up from Aunt Lucy's writing-table and said "Hullo!" She ran to him.

"I want to talk to you. Send her away."

Lee may have heard what she said. She shut the sitting-room door and went into Lucy Craddock's bedroom. She was so stiff and bewildered in her mind that it didn't seem to matter where she went or what she did, except that it was a little better when Peter was there. She sat down on the bed and waited, shivering, although the day was so hot.

In the next room Mavis was talking nineteen to the dozen. What she had said, what the Inspector had said, what she wanted Peter to say—it all came out without pause or stop in a high, excited voice. Peter let her talk herself to a standstill. Then he said calmly,

"You've admitted coming home with Ross. You've admitted hitting him over the head with the decanter and coming across to my flat—"

"Because Miss Bingham saw me," said Mavis.

Peter looked at her with a cynical eye.

" 'You tell the truth because you must, and not because you will.' Parody on Matthew Arnold. No matter. What you haven't admitted is the excursion at three in the morning."

"I didn't," said Mavis in a hurry.

"You didn't admit it? Or you didn't go out of the flat?"

"Miss Bingham made it up. She's a horrid spiteful old cat."

"She says she saw you at three in the morning."

"She made it up," said Mavis in a sullen voice.

"What's the good of saying she made it up? I mean,

what's the good of saying it to me, when you know perfectly well that I saw you come in?''

She shook her head.

"She made it up. You didn't see me."

Peter walked meditatively to the window and back again. Then he said with alarming mildness,

"That is what I am to say at the inquest?"

She gave an impatient nod.

"Of course."

"I am, in fact, to commit perjury?"

"You're not to say you saw me."

His manner changed.

"Look here, Mavis—did you shoot him? You'd much better tell me. If you did, I'll do my best for you."

"I didn't—I didn't! Of course I didn't! Why should I?"

He shrugged his shoulders.

"Half a dozen reasons why you should. But if you didn't, it goes. I wonder if you're speaking the truth. You haven't had an awful lot of practice, have you?"

"Peter, I didn't shoot him—I didn't!"

"Well then, we've all got to tell the truth. Because somebody shot him. As long as it wasn't you the best thing you can do is to weep on the Inspector's shoulder and tell him all. If you lie, he'll find you out. If you hold things back, you'll get tripped up the minute a lawyer gets on to you, and it's a thousand pounds to a halfpenny you'll forget what you've said and say something else, and then the fat will be in the fire. It takes a heap more brains than you've got to be a consistent perjurer. Personally, I intend to stick to the truth."

"You're going to say—you saw me—at three o'clock?"

"I am."

She changed, softened, came up to him caressingly.

"Peter, I only went to find my bag. I told you so."

"Tell the Inspector, my dear."

She put a hand on his shoulder, whispering,

"They've found my dress—it got stained—I cut a piece away. Oh, Peter, they'll think—"

"How did it get stained?"

He held her away and watched her face. She said very low,

"I—knelt—down—"

"You were there?"

She wrenched herself away and sprang back.

"No, no, I wasn't—I wasn't!"

He stood where he was.

"You knelt down beside Ross—after he was shot?"

"No, no, I didn't!"

"I think you did." After a pause he said, "You'd better see a solicitor at once. I can't advise you—it's too serious."

She came up to him again.

"You mustn't say you saw me! Peter, you won't!"

"Look here, Mavis, what's the good of my saying I didn't see you? Miss Bingham saw you. You'd better make a clean breast of it. I shan't say anything unless I'm asked, but I'm bound to be asked."

The door bell rang, and went on ringing. It sounded as if someone had put a finger on the bell-push and was keeping it there. Lee got up wearily off the bed and went to the door.

In the sitting-room Mavis put her lips quite close to Peter's ear and said,

"If you tell about me, I shall tell about Lee—so there!"

CHAPTER

XX

L EE OPENED THE door and saw Miss Phoebe Challoner just putting up her finger to push the bell again. Even on this very hot day Miss Challoner wore a neat tight coat and skirt of clerical grey, and shiny black kid gloves. Her very thick iron-grey hair was drawn back into a plait which she wore coiled round and round at the back of her head. There was so much plait that her hats always sat on the top of her head and tilted forward. They were very neat hats, usually boat-shaped, and trimmed with one of those hard ornaments which look as if they had become accidentally detached from a piece of funerary sculpture.

Miss Challoner had a square, pale face, a stubborn chin, and a pair of steel-grey eyes under very marked eyebrows. She was a friend of Lucy Craddock's, and Lee's heart sank within her, because if Miss Challoner had heard about Ross's death, no power on earth would prise her away from the front door. She would insist on coming in, and she would continue to ask questions until she felt quite sure that she had got all the answers.

Miss Challoner dropped her black kid finger from the bell and said,

"How do you do, Lee? I thought you had gone to America."

Lee shuddered. It wasn't fair that she should have to

confront Miss Challoner on the top of everything else. If she gave her the smallest opening, all would be over. She would find herself sitting down to a cosy *tête-à-tête* and imparting full details of the Merville affair as a preliminary to all about Ross.

She allowed only one word to cross her lips. She said, "No."

"Dear me—how was that? Lucy didn't say. You must tell me all about it. You look terribly washed out. If you find a little heat like this so trying you would certainly not have enjoyed South America. It was South, wasn't it? But I see New York had a temperature of a hundred and five yesterday, so if you feel the heat you had better stay on this side of the Atlantic. But I didn't come here to talk about the weather, I came here to fetch poor Lucy's things." She turned her head sharply and saw Detective Abbott emerge from No. 8. "What's that policeman doing here?"

Lee's original desire to keep Miss Challoner out of the flat changed suddenly to a desperate anxiety to get her inside before she could start cross-examining Detective Abbott. She said all in a breath,

"There's been an accident. Please do come in. What did you say about Cousin Lucy's things?"

Miss Challoner detached her gaze with reluctance. Detective Abbott went back into the flat, but he did not close the door.

"An accident?" said Miss Challoner at the pitch of a naturally strong voice. "Who has had an accident?"

Lee took no notice.

"What did you say about Cousin Lucy? Do please come in. Why do you want her things?"

"Three nightgowns," said Miss Challoner rapidly, "three vests, bedroom slippers, dressing-gown, toothbrush, and a tube of toothpaste."

"Why?" said Lee, staring at her.

"She forbade me to telephone," said Miss Challoner. "When I said, 'I will ring up Craddock House and let them know that you are with me,' she absolutely forbade me to do so, and in her alarming state of agitation I felt obliged to give her the promise she demanded. But nightgowns and a toothbrush she must have, so I have come to fetch them.''

Lee felt quite dazed. She said in a light faraway voice,

''I haven't the least idea what you're talking about. Would you like to tell me—but it doesn't matter if you don't want to.''

''You look extremely washed out,'' said Miss Challoner. ''I can't think why you should be so confused. I find this hot weather very bracing myself. It seems to me quite obvious if poor Lucy is to be confined to her bed for several days, that she will require her nightgowns and a toothbrush.''

Lee took hold of the door jamb. She said as slowly and distinctly as she could,

''Cousin Lucy started for the Continent last night. I saw her off at Victoria.''

''She didn't go,'' said Miss Challoner.

''I saw her off.''

''Did you see her to the barrier, or did you see her into the train?''

''To the barrier, but—''

''She didn't go,'' said Miss Challoner firmly.

''What did she do?'' Lee could only manage a whisper.

''She turned back. As soon as you were gone. She had something on her mind and she felt she couldn't start—something to do with that niece of hers, Mavis Grey. She felt she must see her again before she went. But she couldn't find her. She seems to have gone to and fro looking for her for hours, and she seems to have worked herself into a terrible state of nerves. Really, by the time she came to me she was quite unhinged. Dr. Clarke says she must be kept perfectly quiet and not attempt to get out of bed for several days. I have had to lend her a nightgown, but I always wear flannel, and she dislikes it very much. She has lost her luggage ticket, so I cannot get any of her things out of the cloakroom, and nightgowns and a toothbrush she must have.''

About a third of the way through this speech Lee took her hand off the jamb and stepped back. She tried to draw Miss Challoner with her, and she tried to stem the flow of her words. She might have spared herself the pains. Nobody had ever yet succeeded in interrupting Miss Challoner, and nobody ever would. She merely raised her voice, increased its volume, and pronounced each word more forcibly. What she began to say, that she would finish. She finished.

Lee said in a trembling voice, "Oh, do please come inside," but it was too late.

Detective Abbott came out of Ross Craddock's flat and crossed the landing. He said,

"Just a moment, madam. I think the Inspector would like to see you."

Miss Challoner swung round.

"The Inspector?"

"Yes, madam. I think he would like to know at what hour Miss Lucy Craddock reached you in the agitated state which you have just described to Miss Fenton."

"I can't see what it's got to do with the police," said Miss Challoner briskly, "but I am sure I have nothing to conceal. Miss Craddock knocked me up at a quarter past three this morning."

CHAPTER
XXI

INSPECTOR LAMB SAT at Ross Craddock's writing-table and gazed frowningly at what the fingerprint experts had sent him. The heat of yesterday had turned to heavy cloud and the threat of rain.

"I've taken a dislike to this place, Abbott," he said.

"Did you say 'place,' or 'case,' sir?"

"Both," said the Inspector succinctly. He threw a gloomy glance at the large photograph of Miss Mavis Grey which Peterson's ministrations had restored to an upright position and placed upon the mantelpiece. It had been found on the floor with a crack across the glass and across Miss Grey's slender neck. "That girl's a liar if I ever saw one," he added. "Now look here, I'm going to run over what we've got against the lot of them—just to clear my own mind, as it were. You can take it down."

"Very well, sir."

"Number one—Mr. Peter Renshaw. Plenty of stuff there. He is on bad terms with his cousin. He has words with him about Miss Grey. He is seen just inside his open door when Miss Grey comes back to the flat at three A.M., when, to my mind, there's no doubt at all that the murder had already been committed. *And* he comes in for most of the money. On the top of that we have his suspicious behaviour with the revolver. Apart from this there is no other fingerprint of his inside the flat. Got that down?''

"Yes, sir."

"Number two—Miss Mavis Grey. All her behaviour very suspicious, and a real determined liar. What's the sense of her admitting she was in the flat with Mr. Craddock and ran away from him to Mr. Renshaw, and then denying that she went back to the flat again, when the same witness can swear to having seen her enter Mr. Renshaw's flat on both occasions? Plenty of her fingerprints everywhere—on the glass, on the decanter, on the table that was knocked over, and, for all we know, on the revolver before Mr. Renshaw started playing with it. Why can't she say what she was doing that second time, confound her?''

Detective Abbott looked up.

"It seems to me, sir, that she admits the first visit because she doesn't mind admitting that she hit Craddock over the heat with the decanter, but she won't admit the second visit because she then either shot Craddock herself or saw someone else shoot him."

"Mr. Peter Renshaw?"

"Not necessarily—" He hesitated.

"If you've got anything to say, say it!"

"It was something that struck me as rather curious."

"When?"

"Yesterday—just before I brought Miss Challoner in to you. She was talking to Miss Fenton at the open door of number seven, and Miss Fenton was trying to get her to come in. Well, just as I said that you would like to see her, the sitting-room door opened and Mavis Grey came out. Renshaw was behind her, and I'm pretty sure they'd been quarrelling. Both of them had the look of it, and the girl was in a hurry to get away. Well, this is what I noticed. She was in a hurry, but she wasn't in such a hurry that she would pass Miss Fenton. She would have had to touch her, you know, and she wouldn't do it. She baulked, and when Miss Fenton did move she shied past her just like a horse does when it's scared. I thought it was odd, sir.''

"Might only mean she'd been quarrelling with Mr. Renshaw about Miss Fenton."

Without speaking, Detective Abbott registered a polite rejection of this theory.

The Inspector said somewhat testily,

"Number three is Miss Lucy Craddock. Very suspicious behaviour indeed. She disapproves of Mr. Craddock's attentions to her niece, quarrels with him, and is told she will have to turn out of her flat. Instead of leaving Victoria at seven-thirty-three as she had planned, on a trip to the Continent, she puts her luggage in the cloakroom and goes off to find Miss Mavis Grey. She calls at Mr. Ernest Grey's house in Holland Park at a quarter to nine, and is told that Miss Grey is out. Between then and a quarter past three in the morning, when she arrives at Miss Challoner's flat in Portland Place, we haven't been able to trace her movements. She was probably trying to find Miss Grey. She may have come back here to find her, or she may not. All we know for sure is that she was looking for her, and that when she turned up at Miss Challoner's she was in an unhinged and distracted condition. Her doctor says she won't be fit to make a statement for a day or two. Fingerprints which correspond to what are probably hers, taken from objects in her own flat, have been found on the back of one of the chairs in here. But as Miss Bingham saw her leave this flat in the afternoon that doesn't prove anything."

"She may have wandered in and found him dead. That would account for the shock."

"Then why didn't she raise the house? What would you expect a timid old lady to do? Yell her head off and rouse the house. Why didn't she do it? And I say the answer to that is, either she shot him herself, or she saw the person who shot him and she didn't want to give him away."

"Him—or her—" said Detective Abbott in a meditative voice.

Inspector Lamb looked at him sharply. After a moment he said,

"Number four—Miss Lee Fenton. Nothing against her except these." He tapped a sheet covered with fingerprints.

"The room was fairly plastered with them—both sides of the hall door, both sides of this door, backs of three chairs, and the mark of her whole hand on the corner of this writing-table. Now she couldn't have been in in the afternoon, because she didn't get here till eight o'clock, and then, she says, she had a bath and went straight to bed. Then there are those footprints. Peterson swears that they were the marks of a naked foot and quite distinct when he found the body. By the time he came back with Rush they were nothing but bloodstained smears. Now they weren't Miss Grey's footprints, because she was wearing silver shoes when Miss Bingham saw her—and, by the way, those shoes have never been found, so it's likely they were badly stained. All she'll say is that they were old, and that she threw them away."

"She might have dropped them in the river," said Detective Abbott.

The Inspector nodded.

"She probably did. It's handy, and even if they're fished up now, the stains will be out of them, and we don't get any farther than what she says—that she threw them away. Well, we've rather got off Miss Fenton, but there isn't anything to get back to except those prints—and the way she looks. Talk about shock—that young woman's had one if I'm not very much mistaken."

"She may have been fond of Craddock," Detective Abbott put forward the suggestion blandly.

"Then she was the only one of the lot that was."

"You never can tell, sir."

The Inspector turned over the papers in front of him with a frown.

"The other prints found in here, besides Mr. Craddock's own, are Peterson's, Rush's—he says he was in here speaking to him in the early afternoon—and a set of prints at present not identified—four fingers and a thumb of a man's left hand on the door of this room at a height of four foot seven. That means a man of about six foot. Also the same left-hand print from two places on the banisters—one just at the first turn as you go down, and the other near the bottom.

These prints are very important indeed, as they point to the presence of another person, as yet unidentified, who may have been the murderer. Well, there we are. Go along down and see if that charwoman's come back—what's her name— Mrs. Green. Lintott checked up on her, and the people in the house where she lodges say she came home about half past nine on the evening of the murder so much the worse for liquor that they had to help her to bed. She lay all day yesterday, and she's supposed to be coming back today. Go and see if she's come. There's a point or two I'd like to ask her about.''

CHAPTER

XXII

MRS. GREEN CAME in in her old Burberry with her battered black felt hat mournfully askew. The port-wine mark on her cheek showed up against the puffy pallor of the rest of her face. Her grey hair fuzzed out wildly in all directions. About her neck she wore, in lieu of the crochet shawl reserved for "turns," the aged black feather boa which marked a return to the normal. A sallow handkerchief was clasped in one hand. On being invited to sit down she gulped and applied it to her eyes.

"Thank you kindly, sir. I'm sure it's all so 'orrible, I don't hardly know where I am. And on top of one of my turns too, and this one so bad, and if it hadn't been for the mite of brandy I come by just in time there's no saying whether I'd be here now."

The Inspector relaxed.

"Ah—it takes a good bit of brandy to pull you round out of one of those turns, doesn't it, Mrs. Green?"

Mrs. Green wiped her eyes.

"If it's Mrs. Smith where I lodge that's been telling your young man that I drink, then she's no lady," she said with dignity. "I don't wish her nor no one else to go through the h'agony that I go through when I gets one of my turns, and what they told me in the 'orspital was to take a mite of brandy and lay down quiet, and so I done. And if I'm to get the sack for it, well, it's a cruel shame, and maybe they won't find it so easy to get a respectable woman to come into an 'ouse like this, what with murders and goings on. And if it comes to getting the sack, there's more than me was for it, if it wasn't for Mr. Craddock being done in.''

"And what do you mean by that, Mrs. Green?" said the Inspector.

Mrs. Green eyed him sideways.

"There's those that gives themselves airs and talks haughty now that'd be singing on the other side of their mouth if it wasn't for pore Mr. Craddock lying a mortual corpse at this moment instead of standing up on his two feet and telling them to be off out of here because they wasn't wanted any longer.''

"I really think you had better tell me what you mean, Mrs. Green.''

The sideways look became a downcast one. The pale mouth primmed and said with mincing gentility,

"I'm sure I was never one to put myself forward, sir.''

The Inspector became hearty.

"Pity there aren't more like you in that way, Mrs. Green. But it's everyone's duty to help the police, you know, so I'm sure you're going to tell me what this is all about. If you know of someone who was going to be dismissed by Mr. Craddock, I think you ought to tell me who it is.''

"And him taking it on himself to say as how he'd see to it I got my notice!'' said Mrs. Green with an angry toss of the head.

"Were you alluding to Rush?''

The head was tossed again.

"If it was the last word I was h'ever to speak, I *was*, sir.''

Detective Abbott began to write.

"Rush was under threat of dismissal by Mr. Craddock?''

"I heard him with my own ears, sir, as I was coming across the landing. The door of the flat was open, and the door of this room we're in was on the jar, and Mr. Craddock, he was in a proper shouting rage, and you'll excuse me repeating his language, which wasn't fit for a lady to hear let alone to repeat. He says as loud as a bull, 'You've been mucking up my papers!' he says. And Rush, he answers him back as bold as brass. 'And what would I want with your papers, Mr. Ross?' he says. And Mr. Craddock says, 'How do I know what you want? Blackmail, I shouldn't wonder!' And Rush ups and says, 'You did ought to be ashamed of yourself, Mr. Ross, talking to me like that!' And Mr. Craddock says, 'Get to hell out of here!' And Rush come out, and when he see me, if ever there was a man that looked like murder, it was him, and he went down the stairs swearing to himself all the way.''

The Inspector said, ''H'm! Mr. Craddock had missed some of his papers. Is that what you made of it?''

Mrs. Green sniffed.

''I couldn't say, sir. That's what I heard. I can't say more and I can't say less. What I hears I remembers. And there's more things than that I could tell you if I thought it my duty like you said.''

''It is undoubtedly your duty,'' said the Inspector in a most encouraging voice.

Mrs. Green sniffed again.

''I'm not one to listen, nor yet to poke my nose into other people's business, but I've got my work to do, and if a lady leaves her door open and talks into her telephone that's just inside, well, it's not my business to put cotton wool in my ears. And no later than the very evening before poor Mr. Craddock was murdered what did I hear but Miss Lucy Craddock say—''

''Wait a minute, Mrs. Green. When you say the evening before Mr. Craddock was murdered, do you mean the Tuesday evening? He was murdered some time after midnight of that night.''

''Yes, sir—the Tuesday evening. It would be about a quarter to half past six, and a shocking long day I'd had on account of cleaning up after Mr. and Mrs. Connell.''

''You were on the landing, and Miss Craddock's door was open?''

''Half open, sir. She was all ready to start—going abroad she was—and Rush had just been up for the luggage, when the telephone bell went, and there she was, talking, and never give a thought to the door.''

''Well now, what did she say?''

''You could have knocked me down with a feather,'' said Mrs. Green. ''Dusting the banisters I was, and I heard her say quite plain, 'Oh, my dear, you know Ross is turning me out.' And then something about there being nothing in the will to stop him, and he wouldn't turn Miss Mary out on account of her being an invalid—that's the one that died—but as for Miss Lucy, he said she'd got to go. Getting on thirty years she's been there, and I don't wonder she was put about. She said as how he'd written her a horrible cruel letter, and it was all about Miss Mavis Grey that he didn't mean no good to. Ever so worked up she sounded. And, 'I've got quite a desperate feeling,' she says. It was Miss Fenton she was talking to, and there was a lot about *her* wanting to come here while Miss Lucy was away. I'd my dusting to do and I didn't trouble to listen, but I heard Miss Craddock say as how she was feeling desperate, and desperate she sounded—I'll swear to that. And now they're saying she never went off to the Continent at all. Looks as meek as a mouse she does, but there—it's often the quiet ones that's the worst when they're roused.''

The Inspector let her go after that.

''Every blessed one of 'em might have done it as far as I can see,'' he said in a disgusted tone as Detective Abbott came back after making sure that both doors were shut. ''Talented lot of eavesdroppers they've got in this house too!''

''Yes, sir.''

The Inspector took a decision, a very minor decision, but one that was to have an unforeseen result. Getting out of his chair, he said,

''I'll go down and have a word with Rush. Perhaps he'll be easier to handle in his own quarters. And I'd rather like to see that wife of his. I suppose she *is* bedridden.''

''Haven't you got enough suspects without her, sir?'' said Detective Abbott.

CHAPTER

XXIII

THE RUSHES' BASEMENT room had a fair sized window through the top of which Mrs. Rush could see the railings which guarded the area and the legs and feet of the passers-by. She didn't complain, but she sometimes felt that it would be pleasant to see a whole person for a change. For one thing, she never knew what sort of hats were being worn, and she took a particular interest in hats. It was no good asking Rush, because the vain adornment of their heads by young females was one of the subjects upon which it was better not to set him off.

Everything in the room was as bright and neat and clean as a new pin. Mrs. Rush wore a white flannelette nightgown, and her bed had a brightly printed coverlet. She had finished her baby socks and was starting a little vest for Ellen's baby. On the newly distempered wall opposite her bed hung photographic enlargements of her five children, all taken at about the same age, so that a stranger might have been misled into thinking her the mother of quintuplets. There was Stanley who had been killed on the Somme; Ethel, dead thirty years ago come Michaelmas; Ernie that was in Australia and only wrote at Christmas; Daisy—well Daisy didn't bear thinking about; and Ellen, her youngest and her darling. There they hung, the little boys in sailor suits and the little girls in starched white muslin dresses, and Mrs. Rush looked at them all day long. She had fought the one terrible battle of her married life when Rush wanted to take Daisy's picture down, and she had fought it to a finish and won. "She hadn't done nothing wrong when that was took. That's how I see her, and that's how I'm a-going to see her, and you can't get me from it."

Rush looked surprised and not at all pleased when he saw the Inspector. Mrs. Rush on the other hand was pleasurably excited. It was pain and grief to her to be out of things, and here after all was Inspector Lamb and a pleasanter spoken man you couldn't hope to find. Asking how long she'd been ill, when most people had forgotten that there had ever been a time when she was up and about. Quite a little colour came into her cheeks as she talked to him. And he noticed the children's pictures too, and said he was a family man himself. And no manner of good for Rush to stand there grumbling to himself. Right down bad manners, and he needn't think he wouldn't hear about it when the Inspector was gone.

"Well now, Mrs. Rush, I just want a word with your husband here, and I hope I'm not disturbing you coming in like this, but to tell you the truth I'm right down sick of that room upstairs, and I thought I'd like to make your acquaintance."

He crossed to the foot of the bed and turned to Rush.

"There's a matter that came up just now, and I'd like to know what you've got to say about it. I've been told that you and Mr. Craddock had words on Tuesday afternoon—something about his papers having been disturbed."

"Who said so?" said Rush with a growl.

"Someone who heard what passed. Come, sergeant, tell me about it yourself if you don't want me to take someone else's story."

"Albert—" said Mrs. Rush in a pleading voice.

"There's nothing to tell!" said Rush angrily. "Mr. Ross, he forgot himself. Thirty years I been in this job, and the first time anyone ever said or thought but what I did my duty! Mr. Ross, he forgot himself, and now that he's dead I've no wish to bring it up."

There was a rough dignity about his squared shoulders and the set of his head. "If he isn't an innocent man, he's a very good actor," thought the Inspector. He said,

"That does you credit. But I've got my duty too, you know, and I'll have to ask you what took place between you."

Mrs. Rush looked up from her knitting.

"Now don't you be so disobliging, Father."

Rush scowled at her. A completely meaningless mannerism as far as she was concerned, it having quite ceased to intimidate her after the first month of their marriage.

"A lot of busybodying going on over this business, it seems to me." The Inspector was getting the scowl now. "First and last of it was, Mr. Ross called me into his room and said someone had been mucking about with his papers. Then he forgot himself and said it was me—said there was papers missing, and something about blackmail. And I told him he'd forgot himself and I come away."

"Why should he think it was you? You haven't got a key to the flat, have you? Why didn't he suspect Peterson?"

"No, I haven't got a key—and if I had a hundred I wouldn't touch his papers. But Sunday Peterson had the day off and I had his key. And seems Mr. Ross forgot his bunch of keys that day—left them lying on his table. He's uncommon careless with them. And I told him straight I saw them, and I never touched them nor I never touched his papers, and if anyone says so, alive or dead, he's a liar!"

"Did he threaten you with dismissal?" said the Inspector.

Rush glared at him.

"No, he didn't."

"Sure of that?"

"What are you getting at?"

The Inspector was watching him closely.

"When a murder has taken place, anyone who has had a serious quarrel with the murdered man is bound to come under suspicion."

A deep flush ran up to the roots of Rush's thick grey hair. He breathed heavily. Then he said,

"You're suspecting *me?*"

Mrs. Rush said, "Oh, sir!" She let her knitting fall and clasped her hands. "Oh, sir! Oh, Albert! Oh, sir—he never did! Oh, Albert—you've got to tell him now. It's not right—not if they're going to think it's you. And if he's innocent it won't hurt him, and if he's done it it's not for us to stand in the way of the law—"

"Here," said Rush, "you're upsetting her—that's what you're doing. And I won't have it! Come into the kitchen!"

Mrs. Rush began to tremble very much.

"Not a step!" she said. "Albert, you come right over here and let me get a hold of you!"

"All right, all right—nothing to put yourself about like that, my girl."

She leaned back against her pillows.

"Give him the case, Albert," she said.

"Have it your own way," said Rush.

He opened a drawer, took out a silver cigarette-case, and landed it to the Inspector.

"I was going to give it back to him on the quiet," he said. "Found it laying by the side of the stairs Wednesday morning when I come to do the hall. Didn't think anything about it at first, no more than what he'd dropped it, and I put it away to give it back to him or to Miss Mavis."

The Inspector looked at the case—an ordinary engine-turned affair with a medallion for initials. The initials were R. F. He pressed the catch and the case fell open on his palm. There were cigarettes on one side, but on the other side there was a photograph of Miss Mavis Grey.

The Inspector pursed his lips as if he were going to whistle. Then he said,

"And who were you going to give it back to?"

The porter and his wife spoke together. Rush said, "Mr. Bobby Foster," and Mrs. Rush said, "Miss Mavis's young man."

CHAPTER

XXIV

A BOUT TWENTY MINUTES later the Inspector hung up the receiver and faced Detective Abbott across the writing-table.

"Inquest tomorrow at two-thirty. We'll have 'em all there, and perhaps it'll put the wind up some of 'em. But we shall have to ask for an adjournment unless we get a bit of luck."

"Like the murderer walking in and saying 'Please, sir, I did it.' "

The Inspector frowned.

"Lintott's gone to check up on Mr. Foster. I want his fingerprints. If they correspond with the lot we couldn't account for on the banisters and on this door, then it looks pretty black against him."

"What did the Ducks and Drakes say?"

"Oh, he was round there on the Tuesday night, but he was so drunk they wouldn't let him in. Tried three times—asked for Miss Grey and said he'd got to see her. The porter says Mr. Renshaw put him into a taxi and sent him home. Well, suppose he got home and got drinking some more, and then came round here to have it out with Mr. Craddock—I don't mind telling you it begins to look like that to me. I've told Lintott to find out at his rooms when he came in, and whether anyone heard him go out again—" He broke off because the sitting-room door was pushed open and Peter Renshaw came in.

"Am I interrupting?" he said.

"As a matter of fact I wanted to see you, Mr. Renshaw. I am informed that you met Mr. Foster—Mr. Bobby Foster— as you came out of the Ducks and Drakes on Tuesday night, and that after some conversation you got him into a taxi and sent him home."

"All correct."

"Well now, Mr. Renshaw, I have an account of that conversation from the porter at the Ducks and Drakes. He says Mr. Foster had been backwards and forwards asking for Miss Mavis Grey and wanting to know whether she was there with Mr. Craddock." The Inspector made a significant pause, and then asked, "Was Mr. Foster drunk?"

"It depends on what you call drunk. He was walking and talking, but I didn't take much notice of what he said."

"Ah, but the porter did. He says Mr. Foster used threatening language—says he offered to knock Mr. Craddock's head off and kick it in the gutter—says he used the expression that shooting was too good for him. How's that, Mr. Renshaw?"

Peter groaned inwardly. Bobby would go and say things like that about a man who was going to get himself murdered. Gosh—what a mess! Aloud he said,

"Bobby is a most awful ass, but he wouldn't hurt a fly."

"I take it that he did say those things then?"

"Look here," said Peter, "I don't know what put you on to Bobby Foster, but it's damned nonsense your suspecting him. He was annoyed because his girl had gone out with another fellow, he'd had—well—one or two over the eight, and he was shooting off his face. If you're really going to murder someone you don't go and have a shouting match about it on the steps of a popular night-club with the porter hanging out both ears to listen—well, it's absurd, isn't it?"

Out of the depths of his experience the Inspector commented

on this to the effect that a drunk would do anything—"And I take it, Mr. Renshaw, that you heard Mr. Foster say, 'Shooting's too good for him'—meaning Mr. Craddock."

Peter smiled affably.

"Rather assuming that, aren't you? Now, leaving this somewhat controversial subject, I really came to tell you that I have been talking to my cousin Miss Lucy Craddock."

"You rang her up?"

"She rang me up. She wants to make a statement."

"She *wants* to make a statement?"

"Apparently. It seems to surprise you. She—" he hesitated for a moment—"well, she's a very conscientious person and she thinks she ought to. But she'd had a shock, and she's naturally timid, and—well, in fact she wants me to be there."

The Inspector considered the point.

"I don't see any objection." He considered still further. "I'm very anxious to get a statement from Miss Craddock, and I'm thinking of sending Abbott to take it down. If she's an elderly lady and timid, my coming in on her after a shock and all—well, it might, so to speak, dry her up. But there's something about the young ones, especially if they've got fair hair, that's wonderfully disarming with old ladies. Just bits of lads they think them, and they get the feeling they're setting them to rights. It loosens their tongues a lot, I've noticed."

When they were in a taxi Peter said,

"Look here, Fug, is it possible to have an unofficial conversation with you? I mean, are you on duty all the time, or could there be some sort of a hiatus?"

Abbott shook his head.

"My superior officer has made a point of reminding me that a policeman on a murder case is a policeman all the time—he doesn't, properly speaking, come off duty at all. What did you want to talk about?"

"Nothing, if it's going to be your duty to take it all down in shorthand and decode it for old Lamb. As a matter of fact, it's nothing confidential. It's only—hang it all, man, can't you see what an infernal mess this is for all of us? I thought if we could talk like human beings and get rid of the condemned cell sort of atmosphere it might do both of us a bit of good.''

Fug Abbott looked out of the window.

''I don't take shorthand notes all the time. If you want to talk, talk—only don't forget you're talking to a policeman.''

Peter laughed a little angrily.

''I wasn't going to offer you a nice, neat confession. What I really wanted to do was to talk to you about my cousin Lucy Craddock. You're going to get a statement from her, and I want you to realize what sort of person she is. She's very easily frightened, and when she's frightened she dithers and goes to bits, but—and this is what I want you to get hold of—however frightened she was, or however much in bits, it wouldn't be possible to induce her to tell a lie. She might hold her tongue about something, but what she says will be the truth.''

Abbott said, ''I see.'' What he thought he saw was that Peter was very anxious for him to believe what Miss Lucy Craddock was going to say. He said without any expression in his voice,

''You know what her statement is going to be?''

''No, I do not. Horrible minds you policemen have. She rang me up, and I'll tell you exactly what she said to me. First of all she said she was better, and then she said Mavis Grey had been to see her, and how dreadful it all was, and perhaps she ought to make a statement, but please would I come too, because she was afraid she might get flustered and she would like to feel I was there—'and I won't say any more on the telephone, dear boy, because you never know who may be listening.' There, Fug, I give you my solemn word of honour that that is every word she said as far as I can remember. There's one thing more. I told you that whatever Lucy said would be the truth. Well, one reason for that is that she was brought up to tell the truth, and another is that she definitely wouldn't know how to make a story up. She's got what I call a photographic mind—quite accurate, quite uninspired, no imagination at all. There—that's all. Now tell me why you are a policeman.''

Abbott continued to look out of the window. He said laconically,

"I was reading for the Bar. My father died. There wasn't any money."

"Any prospects?"

"Quite good, I think. I should probably never have got a brief anyway."

CHAPTER
XXV

MISS CHALLONER OPENED the door to them herself, and at once remarked,

"I disapprove of all this very much. Lucy is not at all fit to be worried by the police. Dr. Clarke said she was to be kept extremely quiet. I fail to see how anyone can maintain that making statements to the police about a murder is an occupation suitable for an invalid. However, she insists on seeing you, so I have no choice."

She opened her sitting-room door and ushered them in.

"Well, Lucy, here they are—and if you have thought better of it, I shall insist on their going away again."

Miss Lucy Craddock held out both hands to Peter. She was ensconced upon the sofa, fully dressed, but looking very white and shaky.

"Oh, my dear boy—I am so glad you have come," she said.

Peter kissed her. Her hands clung to his.

"Well, Lucinda, what have you been up to? Look here, if you're going to tremble, Miss Challoner will turn us out. There's nothing to be frightened about. This is Frank Abbott who used to be my fag at school, and he's come to take down anything you want to say."

Lucy Craddock said, "How do you do?" Then she turned to Miss Challoner.

"Phoebe, dear, if you would kindly leave us—"

"Certainly not!" said Miss Challoner. "You are not at all fit to be left with two young men. Suppose you were to feel faint. I shall certainly not go."

"I should prefer it, Phoebe."

Detective Abbott opened the door.

"I am afraid, Miss Challoner," he said, "that it would be quite out of the question for you to remain. I shall do my best not to alarm Miss Craddock."

"I shall inform Dr. Clarke!" said Miss Challoner indignantly. The door closed behind her.

"Dear Phoebe," said Miss Craddock—"she has been so very kind. Now, Mr. Abbott, will you make yourself quite comfortable? I don't know what I ought to do, but you will help me, won't you?" Her voice trembled perceptibly. "I don't have to take an oath, do I?"

"Oh, no, Miss Craddock. Peter will sit by you, and I will bring this chair up to the foot of the couch. I can write on my knee, and all you've got to do is just to tell me what you know about Tuesday evening."

"It wasn't the evening," said Lucy Craddock faintly. "It was the dreadful, dreadful night."

Frank Abbott brought up his chair, opened a notebook, and said in an encouraging voice,

"Now I am quite ready. Just tell me anything you want to."

"It is all so dreadful," said Lucy Craddock. "I don't know where to begin, indeed I don't. You know I was going away on a cruise. We had been having a very sad time with my sister Mary's death—but Peter will have told you—"

"Yes, he knows all that, Lucinda."

"So I was going away—for a little change. Things had been very disturbing and worrying, and my sister had wanted me to go—but then on the other hand I felt as if I ought to be on the spot. It was all so very difficult."

"Well, you started off for Victoria, Lucinda, and we know you got there, because that's where you met Lee and handed her over the key of your flat. She left you at the barrier. Now suppose you begin there and tell us what happened after that.''

"It's so difficult," said Lucy Craddock. "You see, there was a private matter that was very much on my mind, and when it came to the point I felt that I really could not get into the train and go away. I felt that I had not done all I might. It was quite a private matter, Mr. Abbott.''

"My poor Lucinda," said Peter—"nothing is private in this affair. Everyone knows that you were unhappy about the way Ross was running after Mavis.''

"Oh, my dear!''

Peter patted her shoulder.

"I know—but it can't be helped. Brace up! We've all got to get used to living in public. Now get back to where you felt you couldn't go away without having another shot at making Mavis see reason.''

"I felt I *must*," said Lucy Craddock with sudden energy. "I was going to spend the night with Maggie Simpson at Folkestone—Professor Simpson's daughter, a very old friend— so I thought I could see Mavis, and catch an early morning train and cross by the same boat as the others. It was a conducted tour, you know. So I put my luggage in the cloakroom and sent off a telegram.''

"Yes?''

"And then—yes, I think I had a sandwich and some milk, because I didn't want to arrive in the middle of their dinner. And then I started out to go to Holland Park.''

"Mavis Grey lives out there with an uncle and aunt," said Peter.

Abbott nodded.

"Yes—I've got the address. What time did you get there, Miss Craddock?''

"I don't know, Mr. Abbott. It was getting dark. It took me a long time, because I got on to the wrong bus. And when I got there my niece had gone out—so dreadfully disappointing.''

"Darling Lucinda, why didn't you telephone?''

"I never thought of it, my dear.''

"What did you do after that, Miss Craddock?''

"I came round here to see if Phoebe could put me up, but she was out too. She only has a maid in the morning, and there was no one to answer the door, so I went away. And I went into a cinema because I was getting so dreadfully tired, but I can't remember what the picture was or anything about it."

"Why didn't you go home to your own flat, Lucinda?"

Lucy Craddock clasped her hands.

"I felt that I *must* see Mavis—I didn't seem to be able to think of anything else. I stayed in the cinema until it shut, and then I went back to Holland Park and walked up and down waiting for Mavis to come home. I just felt I couldn't go away without seeing her. And then it came to me— suppose she doesn't come home."

"What time was this?" said Frank Abbott.

"It struck twelve, and it struck one, and I kept walking up and down. And then it came to me that Mavis wasn't coming back, and I thought, 'I'll wait another half hour,' so I did, and a little more. And then I knew it was no good, so I went home."

"Home to Craddock House?"

"Yes, my dear. And oh, I do wish I hadn't." Lucy Craddock began to tremble.

Peter put his hand down over hers and steadied them.

"It's all right—you're doing very nicely. You just go on and tell us what happened."

"Do you know what time it was when you got to Craddock House?" said Frank Abbott.

"I don't know, but I think it must have been after two. I must have heard a clock strike two, because I remember thinking how dreadfully late it was, and I got home about a quarter of an hour after that. You see, it took me a long time from Holland Park because I was so very tired and—and distressed, and I think I went out of my way several times."

"Yes," said Frank Abbott. "And at about a quarter past two you came to Craddock House. Was the street door shut? That is one of the things we very much want to know about."

Lucy Craddock pulled herself up on the sofa, pushing away Peter's hand and sitting up clear of the cushions.

"Oh, no—it wasn't shut," she said in an agitated voice. "I had my key all ready, but I didn't have to use it. I saw someone come down the steps, and when I got up to the door I found that it wasn't latched. It upset me very much indeed to think of anyone being so careless."

Peter Renshaw felt a quickening of every pulse. If Lucy had seen someone come out of Craddock House at a quarter past two, then she had probably seen Ross Craddock's murderer.

Abbott said quickly,

"You saw someone come down the steps. Could you see who it was?"

"Oh, no, Mr. Abbott."

"How near were you?"

"I don't quite know—not very near. I had stopped to get out my key, and I saw someone come down the steps quickly—like a shadow."

"Man, or woman?"

"Indeed I don't know. It startled me to see someone coming out of the house so late, but I couldn't see who it was. I wasn't very near, and the porch casts a shadow. I could only see that someone had come down the steps, and when I got there and found the door unlatched—"

"Miss Craddock, this is very important indeed. You say you saw a figure come down the steps. It must have made some impression on you at the time. Shut your eyes and try and think just what you did see—something moving, coming down the steps, coming out of the shadow of the porch, coming down on to the pavement. There must have been a moment when you saw that figure against the light at the corner of the road. Try and think how it looked to you then."

"It's no use," said Lucy Craddock in a shaking voice. "I am short-sighted, Mr. Abbott, and I was very much disturbed at the time."

"Did the figure go away from you towards the corner?"

She shook her head.

"There is a little alleyway between our house and the next one. I think whoever it was must have gone through that way—oh, yes, they must, because I lost sight of them immediately."

Peter said,"You know, Fug, that street lamp is a good way off—it doesn't really light the front of Craddock House."

Frank Abbott sighed.

"Well, we'd better go on. You got to the door, and you found it open—"

"Unlatched," said Lucy Craddock. "And I thought how strange it was, and I went in and shut it after me as quietly as I could because of Mr. Pyne—he sleeps so badly, you know, and always complains that he hears every sound."

"Well, on the one occasion when he might usefully have heard something, he seems to have slept all night. Will you go on, Miss Craddock?"

"I began to go upstairs. The light was on in the hall as usual, but all the landing lights were out. I thought that was very strange indeed."

"You didn't put the lights on?"

"No, I went up in the dark. I thought I would put on the light when I came to my own landing. You see, I had given the key of my flat to Lee Fenton, so I knew I should have to ring and wake her up."

"And did you?"

"No." She sank back against the cushions and clasped her hands again. She said in slow, halting sentences, "I had to find the switch. It is on the wall by the door of Ross's flat. I was feeling for it when I pushed the door and felt it move. I remembered the front door being open, and I was very frightened. It didn't seem to me to be at all right. I opened the door a little way, and there was a light coming from the sitting-room. I called out, and I said, 'Ross, are you there?' "

Her voice quavered in the telling, as it must surely have quavered when she stood in the dark and called to the man who lay dead in the room beyond. She drew a long breath and went on.

"I thought I ought to see if everything was all right. I

went into the hall. The sitting-room door was standing wide open. From where I stood I could see a broken wine glass lying on the floor. There was a horrible smell of spirits and—and gunpowder. I thought about fireworks—and then I thought Ross wouldn't. And then I began to be very, very frightened indeed. I felt as if I must go in, but I was so dreadfully afraid. I had to go in. I was sure something dreadful had happened. I saw Ross lying on the floor—with a pistol in his hand—"

"Miss Craddock, are you sure about that?"

Lucy Craddock began to cry.

"Oh, yes—he was dead—he was quite dead. I saw him—lying there."

"Miss Craddock, *please*. You said just now that the revolver was in his hand."

"Oh, yes—it was."

"Are you quite sure about that? You know, when the body was discovered the revolver was lying some way off."

Lucy Craddock's eyes opened till they looked quite round.

"But I saw it in his hand—and I thought, 'He has shot himself.' And then I thought, 'But why is this door open, and why is the street door open?' And I thought, 'No, he's been murdered, and they've tried to make it look like suicide—because that is what Jasper Crosby did in *Crimson Crime*.' So I am quite sure about the pistol, Mr. Abbott, and if it wasn't there when he was found, then somebody must have moved it afterwards, because he was—oh dear!—quite dead."

"Somebody moved it," said Frank Abbott. "And somebody took care to confuse any fingerprints there might have been."

He looked at Peter Renshaw, and Peter looked back. There was an infinitesimal pause. Then Abbott said,

"Will you tell us what you did next, Miss Craddock?"

"I ran away," said Lucy Craddock simply. "I ran out of the house and down the street. I ran until I couldn't run any more, and then I didn't know where I was. It took me a long time to get to Phoebe's, but at last I did. And then I fainted."

Frank Abbott leaned forward.

"Why didn't you alarm the house?" he said.

Lucy Craddock stared at him. Her chin began to tremble.

"Why didn't you rouse the house? You say you thought your cousin had been murdered. You must have more than suspected that you had just seen the murderer. Miss Fenton and Peter were both within call. Why didn't you call them?"

She went on staring.

"I—I couldn't."

"Why couldn't you? Miss Fenton—Peter—both within call—your own flat waiting for you—why should you run out into the street and wander there for an hour? Why, Miss Craddock?"

She said in a dry whisper,

"I—I was so frightened."

"But you ran way from the people who could have helped you. Miss Craddock, you must have had a reason for running away like that. Shall I tell you what I think that reason was?"

Lucy Craddock said, "No—no."

Abbott went on speaking in his quiet, pleasant voice.

"It was something you saw that sent you running out of the house—I think it was some*one* you saw."

She gasped, and got breath enough to speak firmly.

"No, no, Mr. Abbott, I didn't see anyone—only poor Ross, and he was dead."

He watched her face.

"You didn't see your niece, Miss Mavis Grey?"

"Oh, no, Mr. Abbott."

"Or Miss Fenton?"

A look of simple surprise answered this before she said in a tone of relief,

"Oh, no, not Lee."

"Or—Peter?"

The relief was still in her voice.

"Oh dear, no."

"Miss Craddock, whom did you see?"

"I didn't see anyone—I didn't indeed."

"You saw something that sent you running out into the road. Won't you tell me what you saw? It was something to do with your niece, wasn't it—with Mavis Grey?" He saw her face quiver. "You see, we know she had been there."

She turned at that to Peter, and he said,

"They know that Mavis came back with Ross. He frightened her, and she came over to me at one in the morning. Miss Bingham saw her. Ross was alive then. Miss Bingham, fortunately, saw him too."

Abbott struck in.

"Miss Craddock, you are not helping your niece by holding anything back. A full statement might help her very much, because, you see, she returned to Craddock's flat at three o'clock. Miss Bingham saw her when she was coming back. Miss Grey foolishly denies this second visit and refuses to explain it. But if you saw Ross Craddock dead at a quarter past two, don't you see how important that is to your niece? My idea is that she went back to the flat at three o'clock because she had left something there."

"Her bag," said Peter. "She said she had dropped it on the landing. You know, Fug, she couldn't have expected to find Ross's front door open."

"She may have had a key."

"I don't think so. If she had, it would be in her bag. She had that bag at the Ducks and Drakes, and she didn't have it when she came over to me at one o'clock, but it was in her hand when she came back at three."

"She didn't tell you where she had been?"

"She told me she had dropped the bag on the landing."

"Did you believe her?"

"No."

"Was Craddock's door shut—then—when she came back to your flat?"

"The landing was dark—I suppose Miss Bingham told you that—and I never left my hall, so I don't know whether Ross's door was open or shut. It was shut first thing in the morning."

This rapid interchange of question and answer seemed to pass Lucy Craddock by. When it ceased she said,

"I see what you mean, Mr. Abbott. Indeed that is why I wished to make a statement. If poor Ross had been shot before Mavis went back to that dreadful room to look for her bag at three, then no one could suspect her of having anything to do with it."

"She did go back for her bag then?"

Lucy Craddock looked at him nervously.

"Perhaps I ought not to have said that, but, as I told her, it is our duty to help the law, and he was dead long before she came into the room."

"And it was her bag that you saw, Miss Craddock. Was that it? Was that why you didn't give the alarm?"

"Oh, no, Mr. Abbott. I didn't see the bag at all. I wouldn't have left it there if I had seen it. Oh, no, it had slipped down behind the cushion in that big chair, and I never saw it at all."

"Then what did you see?"

"It was her powder compact," said Lucy Craddock. "It must have fallen off her lap and rolled. It was right at my feet, and of course I knew it at once, because it was a birthday present from Bobby Foster—blue enamel, with her initials on it in diamonds—only of course not real ones, because Bobby couldn't possibly afford that, and I hope Mavis doesn't encourage him to be extravagant."

CHAPTER

XXVI

LEE LOOKED OUT of the bedroom window and saw Peter getting into a taxi with Detective Abbott. Her heart stopped beating, because this meant that Peter had been arrested and was being taken away to prison.

Detective Abbott shut the door with a good resounding bang and the taxi drove away up the street, and round the corner and out of sight.

Lee's heart had begun to beat again, painfully and hard. She hadn't known just how much she loved Peter until she saw him go away like that. She never doubted for a moment that he had been arrested, and if they could arrest him, perhaps they could find him guilty. The most dreadful pictures rushed into her mind, causing her so much agony that she became giddy and had to grope her way to the bed.

But she hadn't time to be giddy. She must do something at once, and she knew just what she had got to do. She ran out of the flat on to the landing and almost bumped into Inspector Lamb. Before he had time to say "I beg your pardon" she had him by the sleeve.

"I want to tell you something! Oh, please, please listen! He didn't do it—he didn't really! I want to tell you!"

The Inspector looked pardonably surprised.

"Steady on, Miss Fenton. What's all this?"

"Please, please listen to me!"

"I'll listen to anything—it's my job. But not out on the landing. There are too many eavesdroppers in this house. Now suppose you ask me into your flat and tell me what it's all about. I'm a bit tired of number eight."

She took him into Lucy Craddock's sitting-room, where he sat down in the big armchair. Lee sat down too, because something seemed to have happened to her knees. She said in a small, rigid voice,

"I want to tell you about Tuesday night. Peter didn't do it—he didn't really. I didn't know you were going to arrest him or I would have told you before."

He looked at her shrewdly.

"I didn't know myself."

"I want to tell you about Tuesday night."

"You have made one statement already, Miss Fenton."

He got an agonized glance.

"I didn't tell you everything."

"Nobody ever does," said Inspector Lamb.

"But I will now—oh, I will really."

The Inspector's second daughter was his favorite, perhaps because she had been delicate as a child. It so chanced that the eyes which gazed at him so imploringly were of the same deep grey as Ethel Lamb's. He coughed, and said in a less official voice than the words warranted,

"If you are thinking of saying anything that would incriminate you, it is my duty to point out that I shall have to take it down, and that it is liable to be used against you."

"Yes—I know. But that doesn't matter at all," Lee said.

She felt a sort of dreadful impatience as she watched him get out his notebook, open it, try the pencil, and very leisurely improve its point. And then she was off on her story, the words tumbling over one another, and every now and then her voice catching and holding them up. Every time the Inspector looked up her eyes were fixed on him with the same desperate intentness. "Are you believing me?" they seemed to say. "Are you—are you? Because you must—oh, you must!"

She was telling him about her father and mother, about

the accident, and how she had walked in her sleep for months afterwards.

"That is years ago. I was only fifteen. I'm twenty-two now. I hadn't done it since, not until Tuesday night."

"And what makes you think you walked in your sleep on Tuesday night?"

All the colour went out of her face as she told him.

"You say your foot was stained, and your nightgown."

"Horribly stained. And then I found my footprints all the way from Ross's door, and the door was shut. I didn't know what had happened. I was afraid to call anyone. I washed my nightgown, and I washed the marks."

"Yes—you shouldn't have done that."

"I was so frightened," said Lee, her eyes wide and piteous.

He went on asking her questions, and to most of them she had to answer, "I don't know."

"You say you woke up with the feeling that something dreadful had happened."

"Yes, but I thought it was in a dream."

"Well, what did you dream?"

"I don't know—I don't remember."

"Nothing at all?"

"No—I never do—I mean, I never did remember anything when I had been walking in my sleep."

The Inspector sat back and looked at her with a frown.

"You know, I don't think this helps us very much, Miss Fenton. All it points to is that whoever shot Mr. Craddock left the door open, and that you walked in your sleep and wandered in there and got yourself messed up." He altered his tone sharply. "Was there any blood on your hands?"

She shuddered and said, "Oh, no—no—not on my hands."

"Well now, Miss Fenton—what do you think about it all yourself? Do you think you shot Mr. Craddock?"

He saw her wince, but she said quite steadily,

"I don't know. Perhaps I did."

"Had you any motive for shooting him?"

"No—not him. But I might have thought he was someone else."

She told him about René Merville.

"He—he frightened me—rather badly. If Ross took hold of me, I might have thought—"

"Did you know Mr. Craddock had a revolver?"

"No, I didn't."

"Have you ever fired a revolver?"

"Why, no."

"Well, suppose you were going to fire a revolver, what would you do? Just tell me. Imagine you've got one in your hand now, and that you're going to fire it at me. What would you do? Go on—tell me."

"I should point it at you, and—and—I should try and aim it."

He nodded encouragingly.

"And then?"

"I suppose I should fire it."

"Well, how would you fire it. Come along—tell me!"

She was frowning now and puzzled.

"I should—press the trigger—you do, don't you?"

"That all?"

Her eyes were perfectly blank.

"I suppose so."

The Inspector burst out laughing.

"Well, you wouldn't find you'd done much damage, Miss Fenton. Ever hear of a safety catch?"

"Yes—I think so."

"Know what it is?"

"Something to do—with a pistol—"

"But nothing that you would have any idea of what to do with. That's about the size of it—eh?"

Lee's lips began to tremble.

The Inspector laughed quite heartily.

"Well, Miss Fenton, I don't think you shot Mr. Craddock. I don't think you'd have known how to set about it even if you had wanted to—and you'd no call to want to that I can see."

"But it wasn't Peter," said Lee, in a tone of misery.

"Well, it looks more like someone else at present," said Inspector Lamb. "And you needn't be so unhappy about him, because we haven't arrested him yet. He's only gone along with Abbott to get a statement from Miss Craddock.''

Quite a bright colour came into Lee's face. She jumped up and stood there breathing quickly.

''And you let me go on and tell you things because I thought you'd arrested Peter! I never heard of anything so mean!''

The Inspector began to say, ''Well, there's no harm done,'' but he broke off in the middle because the door bell was ringing and Lee had gone to answer it. He followed, a little on his dignity. He had been jocose, and when the law unbends it expects appreciation.

The door stood open to the landing, and just outside Mrs. Green was leaning on a broom.

''I thought as how he might like to know the way the telephone bell was ringing in there in number eight, and the door being locked, there's no one can't go in and answer it, not without they've got the key, which I suppose the police has got. And anyhow, seeing I knew the Inspector was in here with you, I thought I'd better ring the bell and let him know.''

Long before the end of this speech the Inspector had his key in the door. The shrill insistence of the telephone bell came to them for a moment before it was muffled and finally cut off.

''There's something about the police in an 'ouse that fair gives you the creeps,'' said Mrs. Green. ''My nerves won't stand it, and that's a fact, Miss Fenton. Badgering you out of your life and suspecting innocent people—that's all they're good for. Good for nothing is what I say, or we shouldn't be murdered in our beds like pore Mr. Craddock.''

''Well, he wasn't in his bed,'' said Lee firmly.

''And well you may so, miss, but that's where he ought to have been at two o'clock in the morning instead of carrying on with those that did ought to know better.''

Lee removed her eyes from the door behind which the Inspector had vanished. It was senseless to imagine that the telephone bell was bound to mean bad news. Anger against herself sharpened her voice as she said,

"You know a lot more about it than I do, Mrs. Green."
Mrs. Green pressed her hand to her side and groaned.

"I'm sure I wish I didn't know nothing," she said gloomily. "My 'ealth isn't strong enough for all this kind of thing, Miss Fenton, and when that there Rush talks about giving me my notice, well, he may think himself in luck's way if he sees me here again, for what with that last turn not being properly gone off, and what with the sight of the police fair turning my stomach, well, I give you my word I haven't kep' down nothing today if it wasn't for a bit of a bloater I made myself take, with a mite of spirits to keep my strength up—and the floor rising under me this minute. Well, I don't suppose I'll be here again, Miss Fenton. There's my pore sister been wanting me this month past, only I wouldn't put no one about, seeing it was holiday time. But if I'm to be misjudged and mistook, well, I'm through, and so I told that Rush just now. 'You can keep your notice to yourself, Mr. Rush,' I said, 'It's me that's giving in mine,' I said. 'Places where gentlemen get murdered and nobody any the wiser—well, they're not what I've been accustomed to, and you can put that in your pipe and smoke it, Mr. Rush,' I said. So you won't be seeing me any more, Miss Lee." Her voice dropped to a carneying tone. She looked sideways and shifted a step or two nearer. "Miss Craddock's been a good friend to me, and pore Miss Mary that's gone. If there was any little remembrance now—" Lee felt a wave of nausea. "There's things I can shut my mouth about, and there's things that I could tell—" The words made hardly any sound. "There's many a little thing I've done—and likely as not you won't be seeing me again—"

Lee lost her temper, suddenly, satisfyingly, and completely. She said, "I'm sure I hope *not!*" and slammed the door upon the offended Mrs. Green.

CHAPTER
XXVII

"WELL, SIR, HERE's her statement," said Detective Abbott. "And if I may say so, I think she was telling the truth. The only thing against it is that Peter Renshaw was particularly anxious to impress upon me beforehand that Miss Craddock was so truthful that she couldn't tell a lie if she tried."

"H'm!" said the Inspector. "He might be very anxious for you to believe that she was truthful, and yet it might be the fact, you know."

"Yes, I know, sir. But you've got to consider the tremendous importance for the whole Craddock family of this point about her having seen someone slip down the steps of Craddock House just before she got there at two-fifteen. If that's true, it lets out Peter Renshaw, Miss Fenton, and Mavis Grey."

"Let's herself out too."

"Yes—only I don't think she needs letting out, really. I'm quite sure her statement is true in the main. I'm certain she did try to find Mavis Grey and make a last appeal to her, and that the reason she didn't give the alarm when she found Ross Craddock lying dead was that she saw Mavis's powder compact and was so frightened at the idea of her being mixed up in the murder that she just panicked and ran away. That's all natural enough. But that shadow slipping down the steps sticks in my throat, and if there's no corroboration, I shouldn't expect a jury to swallow it either."

"We haven't got as far as a jury," said the Inspector. After a pause he added the word "Yet."

He picked up Lucy Craddock's statement and read it through to the end. Then he said,

"What's made her so worked up about this affair between Mr. Craddock and Miss Grey? That's what I'd like to know. Seems to me it's all a bit out of reason. She mightn't like him, and she mightn't want her niece to marry him, but she wasn't even Miss Grey's guardian, and I don't see why she put herself in such a state as this amounts to." He tossed the statement down upon the table. "To my mind there's something behind it, and I'd like to know what it is."

"Yes, sir—you're perfectly right. I pressed her about it, and I think I got something. Craddock couldn't marry Mavis Grey because he was married already."

"*What?*"

"Miss Craddock was a bit incoherent, but I gather that there had been some sort of a war marriage—old history— many years ago—very upsetting for the whole family. The woman was an actress and older than he was, but he was over twenty-one at the time and they couldn't get the marriage upset. It didn't last any time to speak of, but Miss Craddock said she was quite sure there had never been a divorce. She said she didn't think Craddock wanted a divorce, because it suited his book to philander around and then be able to say that of course he hadn't any intentions, because he was a married man."

"Anything known about the wife?"

"I gather that none of them has ever seen her. Miss Craddock says that during the lifetime of her cousin, the elder Mr. Craddock, a small allowance was paid to her through Mr. Prothero, the family solicitor, but she believes Ross Craddock stopped it. There was a thing that struck me there, sir—once I'd got her started Miss Craddock fairly poured all this out. I couldn't help wondering whether this rather mythical wife wasn't a red herring. And that's making me wonder whether Miss Lucy is quite the truthful innocent that Peter wants to make me think she is. First she sees a very convenient shadow slip down the steps of Craddock House, then she says she finds the front door open, and lastly she releases a whole news-reel about a twenty-year-old marriage.''

"I thought you said you believed she was telling the truth.''

Detective Abbott ran his hand back over his hair.

"I know I did. That's the funny thing—when I was talking to her and taking down that statement I could have sworn it was all straight, but the moment I come to go over it to you I can see how fishy it looks. It's too convenient for the Craddocks—that's how it strikes me. And that story of someone coming down the steps—look how beautifully vague she leaves it. It might be a man, it might be a woman—she only says it was someone. And there's no corroboration.''

The telephone bell rang. The Inspector lifted the receiver, listened for a while, and then said,

"That's good enough—we'll pull him in. Good work, Lintott! I'm coming straight over.''

He hung up and turned a satisfied face on Abbott.

"That was Lintott. He rang up whilst you were out to say he'd got a lot of stuff about Foster, and a number of good fingerprints from his brushes and shaving tackle. Foster wasn't there, but he'd got a search warrant. I told him to rush the fingerprint business through and let me know the result. That was it, and it's good enough to put Mr. Bobby Foster in the dock. His prints correspond exactly with the ones we couldn't place, on the banisters and the sitting-room door. He was here that night, and he made those marks and he dropped his cigarette-case. His landlady says he came back in a taxi about midnight and made a lot of noise on the stairs. She says he didn't go to bed, but walked up and down in his room talking to himself and kicking the furniture. Her husband went in to him at half past one and told him he was disturbing the whole house. The man says Mr. Foster was in an awful state—told him his girl had thrown him over, and he was going to buy a revolver and shoot himself, but he was going to shoot the other man first. He says there was a bottle of whisky on the table and Mr. Foster kept pouring himself out another drink. He says he tried to calm him down, but it was no good, and all of a sudden Mr. Foster shouted out that he wasn't going to stand it any longer. 'I'll have it out with him,' he said, 'if I have to blow his head off!' and with that he was down the stairs and out of the house and no stopping him—and by all accounts they were glad enough to be rid of him. They went to bed again, but they didn't bolt the street door. Round about three in the morning the man heard something fall. He opened the bedroom door, and there was Mr. Foster on the stairs in his stocking feet with one shoe in his hand and the other where he'd dropped it on the half-landing. He didn't look drunk any more, but he looked worse. The man says he looked as if he had seen a ghost. And he went back and picked up his shoe and on up to his room, all without making a sound. I'll say we've got our man all right, or will have as soon as I get that warrant. There's no doubt what happened, to my mind. He got round here somewhere about two o'clock, quarrelled with Mr. Craddock, and threatened him. Mr. Craddock had had a bang over the head already and he wasn't feeling too grand. He gets scared, or wants to scare the other man, opens this drawer, and pulls out his revolver. Mr. Foster gets it from him—he's a very powerful young man—and, either in a struggle or deliberately, Mr. Craddock is shot. Mr. Foster throws down the pistol and gets away just as Miss Craddock comes along. It fits in well enough with what she says she saw."

"She says she saw the pistol in Ross Craddock's hand."

"Well, isn't that where Foster would put it if he'd any sense in him at all?"

"He might. There's one thing though—Miss Craddock had a key to the front door of Craddock House, but Bobby Foster hadn't."

The Inspector looked at him, frowning.

"You mean?"

"How did he get in, sir?"

CHAPTER
XXVIII

"WHEN WILL YOU marry me, Lee?"
Peter stood on the hearth-rug and surveyed her with frowning intensity. His hands were thrust deep into his pockets. His tone was business-like and his manner abrupt.

Lee said, "I haven't said I'm going to marry you at all."

His frown deepened.

"Of course you're going to marry me. I do wish you would stick to the point."

"I said I hadn't promised to marry you. That is the point."

"No, it isn't. We settled that yesterday. The present point is, *when* are you going to marry me? And I think it had better be as soon as possible. This is Thursday, and the licence business takes three days. . . . Damn! that means the week-end comes in, so I suppose it will have to be Monday— or will a parson marry you on a Sunday? I don't see why he shouldn't—in the afternoon."

Miss Fenton had a clear and pretty voice. She raised it perceptibly.

"Peter, I am not going to marry you—either on Sunday or Monday. I haven't said that I am going to marry you at all."

He swooped, pulled her up out of her chair, and held her at arm's length.

"Why?"

"It's not—it's not a time to get married."

"My child, marriage isn't a beano. But I see your point. The inquest is tomorrow, and then I suppose they'll let us get on with the funeral, say Saturday, and what's to prevent our getting married on Monday? You want someone to look after you, you know. I can't so much as go out for an hour or two but you go pouring confessions into old Lamb's fortunately unresponsive ear. Poor old Lamb—first he thought Mavis had done it, then it looked as if I was a dead snip until Lucinda dropped on him out of the blue, on the top of which you came along with a confession, and now I gather that he's quite sure it's Bobby. But to return to our licence. You need looking after, I want to look after you, and—"

She shook her head.

"Peter, it won't do—not till this is all cleared up. Don't you see that if you marry me, the police will think I knew something and that you'd done it to make sure I couldn't be called as a witness against you?"

Peter let go of her rather suddenly.

"What a perfectly horrible mind you've got!"

"Well, isn't that just what they would think?"

"I don't know—I suppose they might."

He took her by the elbow and began to walk her up and down the room.

"Look here, my dear, you say put off getting married until the mess is cleared up. But suppose it isn't cleared up—suppose it's never cleared up. Do you realize that we are all under suspicion and we shall go on being suspected till kingdom come unless they really do find out who murdered Ross, and, what is more, prove it up to the hilt? Do you think Mavis did it? I don't. I don't suppose she's ever handled a revolver in her life. Besides, look at what she did earlier on when he got fresh with her. She upped with the decanter and hit him over the head. Very nice, natural, womanly reaction. If she'd had a revolver handy she'd have hit him over the head with it or heaved it at him, but I'll go bail she wouldn't have fired it.''

Lee nodded.

"Yes, I think so too.''

"Always agree with me, darling. You'll find it a splendid foundation for our married life. We now come to me. Do you think I did it?''

"No.''

"I suppose there are circumstances in which I might have done it—I don't know. But whoever shot Ross shot him sitting. That's the medical evidence—the shot travelled downwards. He was shot sitting, probably whilst he was still dazed after the clip on the head Mavis gave him with the decanter. I don't see myself doing that somehow.''

Lee said "No" again.

"Then there's Lucinda. I don't know if they believe her statement, but I do. Of course the wish is probably father to the thought, because if she really did see someone coming out of Craddock House at a quarter past two in the morning, it spreads quite a lot of whitewash over the Craddock family. And that's the snag—they may think the whitewash altogether too convenient.''

"I suppose so. I—I've been awfully frightened about Lucy, Peter. She was most frightfully worked up about Ross, and she doesn't really seem to have known what she was doing on Tuesday night. The thing that frightens me is that as far as I can see she was the only person who could have got in from outside after Rush locked up. She says she found the door open, but—''

"Mavis and Ross came in. They may not have shut the door properly. No—that won't wash. I don't believe anyone could forget to shut a door they'd just opened with a latchkey. You see, he took the latchkey out all right. It was there on his chain. He simply couldn't have forgotten the door. Besides Mavis was there.''

"Then who opened it? Someone did, if Lucy's story is true. Oh, Peter, it frightens me.''

"I know, but you're not going to make me believe that

Lucinda shot Ross. What about Miss Bingham? There's a really bright idea!''

Lee's laugh was half a catch of the breath.

''Peter, I had her here for an hour after the Inspector had gone, and it was *the* very last straw. Talk about third degree!''

''I begin to feel quite sure she did it,'' said Peter firmly. ''She had a secret passion for Ross, and she slew him because he wouldn't reciprocate. Why, she admits being on the spot at or about the fatal time. I believe we have her sleuthed. Call me Renshaw no more—I am Hawkshaw the Detective. I must ring up old Lamb and tell him all before he goes and arrests me, or Lucinda, or the unfortunate Bobby.''

All this time he had been walking Lee up and down, with the pace getting faster and faster, until at its climax he stopped suddenly and embraced her after the French manner, with clasping arms and a kiss upon either cheek.

''Peter! Don't be so mad!''

She got an injured stare.

''Is it that you are offended? Is it not that one is permitted to salute one's betrothed? Do you not love me passionately?''

''No, I don't! And if you think that's a French accent, it isn't!''

He let go of her and ran his hands through his hair.

''All right, let us return to the prison house. We are now going to be very, very serious, and I expect we had better sit down.''

He drew two chairs together and sat forward with his elbows on his knees and his chin in his hand.

''Lee, did you know Ross was married?''

Her eyebrows went up.

''Was he?'' she said. ''I'm not really surprised, you know. Lucy used to drop hints. I suppose that was why she was in such a flap about Mavis.''

''You think Mavis knew?''

''Well, you'd think Lucy would have told her if she wanted to put her off.''

''You'd think so. Well, she told Abbott, and I dropped in

on old Prothero on my way back, and he told me all about
it. She was an actress in a small way—name of Aggie
Crouch, but her stage name was Rosalie La Fay. Ross
married her on one of his leaves in nineteen-seventeen. He
was over age and *compos mentis*, and she was a perfectly
respectable girl, so Uncle John had just to swallow her
down. But by the time the Armistice came along Ross was
through and they separated. Uncle John made her an allowance of three hundred a year on condition she kept out of
everybody's way. Somewhere about nineteen-twenty-five he
reduced it to two hundred—he'd had some losses—and in
nineteen-thirty-one it came down with a run to a mere fifty.
Prothero says it was all he could manage. When he died four
years ago Ross cut it down to twenty-five, and a year ago he
stopped it altogether. You know he really was a swine, Lee.
The woman wrote the most imploring letters—said she
couldn't get a job, and wouldn't he do something for her?
Prothero tried to persuade him, especially in view of the fact
that all the leasehold property was due to fall in and he
could quite easily have let her have the original three
hundred a year again, but he wouldn't hear of it. By the
way, she'll come in for most of that property now."

"What!"

"Bit of a turn of the wheel, isn't it?"

"I thought it came to you."

"What came from my grandfather comes to me. He left it
like that in his will. But most of those leaseholds came to
Ross from his mother without any settlement, and the wife
will get all that. Prothero says that was one reason why he
was so anxious that Ross should make a will. He said he
wrote to him urging him on these very grounds only last
week, and he says Ross had half agreed to do something
about it, but it didn't get any farther than that."

"Does she know?" said Lee.

Peter nodded.

"Prothero wrote yesterday, and she rang him up this
morning from Birmingham. He said she sounded very
upset, and wanted to know when the funeral was, and would
he advance her some money at once, because she would like

to send a really classy wreath. He was rather relieved to know that she had got his letter, because, I gather, she never stays anywhere more than about a month, and he wasn't quite sure whether he'd got the right address.''

"I suppose—" said Lee, and then she hesitated. "Peter, it is beastly to think of these sort of things, but—do you suppose she knew—about the money, I mean?"

Peter shook his head.

"My child, I'd love to suspect Aggie, but I'm afraid it can't be done. You see, she couldn't possibly have known that Ross hadn't made a will, and if he had, she could bet her boots she wouldn't get a penny. All very vindictive and anti-social our cousin Ross's views on matrimony. Anyhow, she was in Birmingham—at least I suppose she was—old Lamb might be asked to check up on that. I did have the bright thought that Miss Bingham might be Aggie in disguise, with an accomplice in Birmingham telephoning to old Prothero, but I'm afraid she's been here too long for that. No, I don't think we can fix it on Aggie.''

Lee said in a shaken voice,

"Peter, who do you think did it really?"

"Any of us, my dear—you, me, Mavis, Lucinda, Peterson—no, I don't really think it was Peterson somehow—old Rush—or what about the bedridden wife—she mayn't really have been bedridden at all, you know—Bobby, Miss Bingham—you pays your money and you takes your choice.''

"No, but *really*, Peter."

"Oh, Miss Bingham without a doubt," said Peter cheerfully.

CHAPTER

XXIX

THE INQUEST TOOK place at half past two on Friday afternoon. No adjournment was asked for by the police, and the jury arrived without difficulty at a verdict of wilful murder against Robert Foster. Indeed, after the evidence of the hall porter at the Ducks and Drakes, reluctantly corroborated by Mr. Peter Renshaw, and the very voluble testimony of the unfortunate Bobby's landlady, Mrs. Nokes, and her husband, they could hardly have done anything else. The cigarette-case was produced and identified and the fingerprints sworn to. No young man could have done more to put a rope about his own neck. Three witnesses to swear to a threat to shoot Ross Craddock. Fingerprints on the banisters of Craddock House and on the door of the room in which the murdered man had been shot. His cigarette-case picked up in the hall. Absence from his room at the material time, between one-thirty and three in the morning. And, most damning of all, the strong motive of jealousy acting on a mind unbalanced by drink. A very neat case, the only thing lacking to complete it being the person of Robert Foster.

"That ass Bobby's done a bunk," said Peter in Lee's ear after a brief interchange of words with the Inspector. "Old Lamb's as sick as mud—says somebody must have tipped him the wink, and I rather gather that he thinks it was me.

As I said to him, however much I wanted to, I couldn't very well have given away what I didn't know myself, and as no one told me that Bobby had been plastering the whole place with fingerprints and dropping cigarette-cases, I don't very well see how I could have blown the gaff. I thought he was just in the same old boat as the rest of us on account of having let off a lot of hot air about Ross outside the Ducks and Drakes, but I'm afraid there's more to it than that.''

"Ssh!" said Lee. "They're going to begin."

Peter's heart warmed to Inspector Lamb when he found that Miss Lee Fenton was not to be called as a witness.

Miss Mavis Grey was called, but failed to answer to her name.

Lucy Craddock gave her evidence faintly but steadily.

Yes, she had seen someone come down the steps of Craddock House as she approached. The time would be about two-fifteen A.M. No, she could not say whether the figure she saw was that of a man or a woman. It was just a dark moving shadow. She was quite sure she had seen someone. She was quite sure that the street door was ajar when she came up to it. And so forth and so on, keeping steadily and exactly to her statement. She turned giddy once, and was given a glass of water which she kept clasped in her black-gloved hand, sipping at it from time to time, but her narrative remained clear and made a visible impression on the jury.

Miss Bingham enjoyed herself a little too obviously, and deprived her evidence of its full effect. Juries do not care for a biassed witness.

If Mavis Grey had been in court, she would have profited to a considerable extent from the malice of Miss Bingham's attack. A pretty girl and a spiteful old maid—the picture could hardly have failed of its effect. But Mavis Grey was not in court. Mavis Grey, a most material witness, was not in court. Mavis Grey was absent, and so was Bobby Foster. Mavis Grey and Robert Foster. Robert Foster and Mavis Grey. A verdict of wilful murder against Robert Foster. Warrants out against Robert Foster and Mavis Grey.

Peter and Lee took Lucy Craddock back to her own flat.

"Dear Phoebe is very kind, but I told her I must come home."

She cried all the way back in the taxi, but her chief concern seemed to be for the presumably unchaperoned flight of Mavis and Bobby.

"And I suppose it will be quite impossible for them to arrange to get married if the police are looking for them. Oh, my dear, it is really all quite dreadful, and I can only feel thankful that poor Mary was spared."

She continued to weep whilst Peter paid off the taxi, whilst Lee gently encouraged her into the lift and out of it again, and during all the preparations for tea. She took two lumps of sugar, and sipped and sobbed, and sobbed and sipped again.

"I can't think why Mavis should have run away," she said between the sips and the sobs—"I really can't. You see, she came to see me yesterday, and we had such a nice talk—at least you know what I mean, Peter dear. The subject couldn't very well be nice, because of course we had to discuss poor Ross being shot—very distressing indeed, even if one wasn't as fond of him as one would like to have been, but you can't be fond of people just because they are going to be murdered—can you—even if you know beforehand, which of course you don't."

Peter patted her on the shoulder.

"Full stop and close the inverted commas. Now take a good long, deep breath and begin again. You had a nice conversation with Mavis, and it wasn't the subject that was nice. What was it, then?"

"Dear Mavis quite opened her heart to me—A little more tea, Lee dear, and not quite so much milk—no, dear, not three lumps of sugar—two will do very nicely. How refreshing tea is. You see, Lee dear, she thought that you had shot poor Ross."

Lee set down the teapot and gazed at her.

"Mavis thought that? Why?"

"Well, she saw you there, my dear. She sat down and burst into tears and told me everything. I am afraid she has been very foolish indeed, only—only—nothing *really* wrong, thank God. I don't wish to speak evil of the dead, but poor Ross ought to have known better—his own cousin, and he couldn't marry her because of Aggie Crouch all those years ago, and there wasn't even a divorce.''

"Be calm, Lucinda—you're getting tied up again."

Lucy Craddock blew her nose on a handkerchief with a narrow black border.

"It wasn't as if Mavis didn't know he was married either, for I felt it a *duty* to let her know."

Peter looked at Lee and saw how pale she was.

"Tell us what happened on Tuesday night," he said firmly—"what Mavis told you. We know she threw over Bobby and went to the Ducks and Drakes with Ross, and then came back here with him, after which she biffed him with a decanter and swooned all over me."

"Oh, my dear boy, she thought I was here—she did indeed."

"I can't think why she should. We all knew you were pushing off on Tuesday, but I suppose Mavis is mutt enough for anything. Now, Lucinda, the biffing and the swooning took place soon after one A.M. At three o'clock both Miss Bingham hanging over banisters and myself in hall of flat saw Mavis come in off the landing. She said she'd been picking up a bag. Police, self, and Miss Bingham all quite sure she had been back to Ross's flat. Suspicion a good deal concentrated on Mavis until you made statement to the effect that you found Ross dead at a quarter past two. I suppose that's why you made it."

Lucy Craddock looked shocked.

"Oh, my dear boy, it was perfectly true."

"Yes, but you made it to clear Mavis all the same. Now what did she tell you? I pushed her off into Mary's bedroom at about twenty minutes past one. What happened between that and three o'clock?"

Lucy Craddock dabbed her eyes.

"Poor dear Mavis—she was very unhappy and very frightened, because, you know, Ernest and Gladys Grey are so *very* strict, and they thought she was with Isabel Young. She threw herself down on the bed just as she was and cried her eyes out. And she must have fallen asleep. She said she woke up very stiff and uncomfortable. She still had her dress on, but she thought she would take it off and go to bed properly. So she put on the light, and when she wanted the face-cream out of her bag the bag wasn't there, and it came over her that she had left it in Ross's flat. At least, what she hoped was that she had dropped it on the landing, but when she went out and looked it wasn't there.''

"Was the landing light on?" said Peter quickly.

"No, it was all dark, just like it was when I was there at a quarter past two. The switch is by Ross's door, and she went over to put it on, and then she saw that Ross's door was open, and the light on in the sitting-room.''

"Both doors open? Did you leave them like that, Lucinda?"

"Yes, I did. But I didn't leave the light on. I couldn't leave it shining down on him like that.''

"But Mavis found it on?" Lee said the words almost in a whisper.

"Yes, my dear, she found it on. And she came into the room, and there was Ross lying dead on the floor just as I had seen him—and oh, my dear, you were standing over him in your night-dress with that dreadful pistol in your hand.''

"She walks in her sleep," said Peter quickly. "She didn't remember anything about it afterwards, but her foot was stained, and her nightgown, and she's been going through tortures ever since because she didn't know what to think.'' He took Lee's hand and held it hard. "Darling, do stop looking like that! Lucinda found Ross dead a good half hour before you walked in on him, and old Lamb proved to you that you couldn't have fired that revolver if you'd tried.''

Lucy Craddock nodded.

"But of course it was quite natural for poor dear Mavis to think what she did. You see, she saw you with the pistol in your hand, and she was too frightened to scream. She wanted to run away, but she simply couldn't, and then she saw that you weren't seeing her at all, and she realized that you were walking in your sleep. She said she didn't know what to do, because she really did think you had killed

Ross. And all at once you turned away and let the pistol fall out of your hand, and then you came walking past her and out of the flat. She heard you cross the landing and shut my door. Well, then she went over to Ross, and knelt down by him, and took his hand to see if he was really dead. And he was. Oh, my dear boy, she was braver than I was, for I couldn't have brought myself to touch him. And when she was sure about that she said to herself, 'Oh, I must find my bag, or they'll think I did it.' And it had slipped down between the cushion and the side of the chair. That is why I didn't find it when I was there—only the powder compact, which had fallen off her lap and rolled. And when she got back to Mary's flat—oh, my dear boy—there you were!''

Peter gave a short laugh.

''And there was Miss Bingham hanging over the banisters and fearing the worst.''

''I have never really liked her,'' said Lucy Craddock. ''She asks so many questions, and if you don't tell her, she finds out just the same. And I'm afraid, my dear boy, you spoke very harshly to poor Mavis. She was dreadfully upset because her dress had got stained when she knelt down by Ross, and she was afraid that you would notice it. She cut out the stained piece and burned it—''

''Yes, and left the rest of the dress pushed in amongst Mary's clothes for the police to find. You know, Lucinda, I honestly don't think that Mavis has got a brain, or if she has, it is definitely sub-human.''

Lucy Craddock shook her head.

''A pretty girl like Mavis doesn't need to have a brain, my dear. Gentlemen really prefer it.''

''And that brings us back to our starting-point,'' said Peter. ''The brainlessness of Mavis may be the reason why she has disappeared, but for the life of me I can't see—''

''You don't think she's eloped with Bobby?'' said Lee.

''Well, I don't know. Up to Tuesday, when everyone would have liked her to get engaged to Bobby, Mavis wouldn't look at him. Would a warrant for his arrest make her feel that she loved him passionately and must incontinently elope?''

"It might," said Lee.

He looked at her, and she blushed.

"Meaning that if they arrest me, you will marry me at the gallows' foot."

"My dear boy!" said Lucy Craddock in a horrified voice.

Peter laughed.

"Well, I don't think Mavis would. Anyhow, here are the facts. Bobby went off to his stockbroking office as usual on Thursday morning. Then he went out to lunch and never came back. By the time old Lamb had made up his mind to arrest him he wasn't there to be arrested, and so far he hasn't been traced. A ham-headed mutt, but I still don't think he shot Ross. Now our cousin Mavis was all present and correct on Thursday. She had breakfast, dinner, lunch and tea in the Grey *ménage*, a good deal of the time being taken up with painful family scenes of the first magnitude. A happy English home!"

"It is no good being too strict with young people," said Lucy Craddock. "And I am afraid it wasn't a very happy home."

"Well, she was still there on Friday morning. She had been served with a summons for the inquest, and Uncle Ernest and Aunt Gladys were preparing to support her through the ordeal. She went out for what Aunt Gladys described as a breath of air at about eleven o'clock, and nobody has seen her since. I can't make that fit in with Bobby at all. I think she was fed up with Aunt Gladys and Uncle Ernest, and she lost her nerve and bolted."

Fresh tears started from Lucy Craddock's eyes.

"Oh, my dears—you don't think she has done something dreadful!"

Peter's eyebrows went up. He said in the voice she liked least,

"In plain English, has she committed suicide? Calm yourself, Lucinda. Mavis is a great deal too fond of Mavis to let her run the very slightest risk. She really does love her, you know, and I'm quite sure she will do her very best to look after her and keep her safe. She won't be very clever about it, but you can't blame the poor girl for that. She'll do her best. Anyhow, she appears to have cashed a cheque for fifteen pounds before she left, and if she'd been going to jump into the river she wouldn't have done that.''

"Oh, my dear, I'm so thankful," said Lucy Craddock. She dabbed with her handkerchief. "Lee dear, I could do with another cup of tea."

CHAPTER
XXX

THE FUNERAL TOOK place next day. Since Lucy Craddock insisted on attending, Lee could do no less. The utmost efforts to keep time and place from becoming known had not prevented a crowd from assembling. Lucy wept, Lee looked as if she was going to faint, and Peter wondered when they would all stop living in a nightmare and be able to return to the decencies of private life.

When it was over he went to see Inspector Lamb, and came back from the interview a good deal depressed in spirits.

"I thought I was on the ground floor, but there's a basement, and old Lamb has just let me down into it with a bump."

He cast himself down on the floor beside Lee and laid his head against her knee.

"You don't feel as if you'd like to kiss me and say a few nice womanly things like 'Darling, we've still got each other,' and, 'It is always darkest before the dawn'?"

Lee smiled a little wanly.

"Peter, if I kiss you I shall probably begin to cry, and that would be about the last straw, because Lucy never stops, does she?"

"I shall divorce you if you cry."

"You can't divorce me till we are married."

Peter pulled down one of her hands and put his cheek against it.

"'A Bride's Cynicism, or Modern Outlook on Marriage,'" he remarked. "You know, if Lucinda heard you talk like that, she'd have a fit. You've got a lovely, soft, cool hand."

"Have I? I'm glad. What did the Lamb say that cast you down into a basement?"

"He'd had a report from Birmingham—about Aggie, you know—and it's no good. She's got a room in quite a respectable sort of lodging-house—been there about a week—and the police and at least three people are prepared to swear that she was there on Tuesday night, because she was taken ill and waked the landlady up at two in the morning, and the husband—the landlady's husband, not Aggie's—went round and knocked up a chemist to get some stuff made up for her. Some kind of a heart attack, and she'd run out of what she takes for it."

"That seems very convenient," said Lee slowly.

Peter twisted round so that he could look at her.

"Do you think it's too convenient?"

She drew a long breath.

"I don't know, but—two in the morning is such a frightfully difficult time to have an alibi for. Why should Aggie have one? It—it—feels queer to me."

He sat right up.

"Darling, your head's going round. Aggie was in Birmingham on Tuesday night having a heart attack unless (a) her respectable landlady, (b) her respectable landlady's respectable husband, and (c) one Mrs. Coltham, who had the room next door and helped minister to the afflicted, are all perjuring themselves black in the face, and really there's on reason why they should, because none of them had so much as set eyes on her a week before. They weren't very enthusiastic about her either. Miss La Fay—she's stuck to her stage name by the bye—Miss La Fay gave a good deal of trouble. They had nothing against her, but theatrical ladies weren't really in their line, they said. So there we are—Aggie Crouch alias Rosalie La Fay is a wash-out. I shall have to concentrate on Miss Bingham.''

"There isn't any news about Bobby Foster, I suppose?"

"Not yet. But it's only a matter of time—they're bound to get him. Besides, if there's anything stupid he can do he'll probably do it, and so will Mavis. There's no news of her either.''

"You know," said Lee, "I think Bobby did it. I mean, he wouldn't if he'd been sober, but if he was pretty far gone when you sent him home at twelve, he probably didn't in the least know what he was doing by two in the morning. He seems to have gone on having one drink after another, and by the time he got round here—well, he mightn't really have known what he was doing, and all those things he'd been saying about knocking Ross's head off and shooting him—don't you see, the idea might have taken charge. People who wouldn't hurt a fly when they're sober do horrible things when they're drunk.''

There was a knock on the outer door. Peter got to his feet.

"If it's a policeman, Lucy's lying down, you are completely prostrated, and I am raving. I shall give an exhibition performance of biting the hall linoleum.''

"I can't bear another policeman," said Lee—"I really can't—not even the Pet Lamb.''

It wasn't a policeman. It was Rush in his Sunday suit, and the black tie he had worn for the funeral. He was clothed in dignity and gloom, and had in his hand a small brass tray entirely covered with keys. The minute the door was fairly open he began upon a speech which bore every sign of having been rehearsed.

"Seeing as you're master here now, Mr. Peter, and the police cleared out, thank 'eavens, I should like to know what about me and what about the keys. All here present and correct except Miss Lemoine's that she's took away with her, number four, and the Miss Holdsworths, number three, and Mrs. and Miss Tatterley, number two. They've taken theirs, though I've always said and always tells them that it's not safe. Suppose there was a fire. Suppose there was these cat-burglars. 'Elpless—that's what we should be.

But all the others is here. Lady Trent, number six—I'll say that for her, she always 'ands hers in and no bones about it. And Potters, ten and eleven, and Connells, number five— they left theirs with Mrs. Green for her to clean up after them. And that's another thing that didn't ought to be done, and I'd like to get that straight with you here and now, Mr. Peter—keys is my responsibility, and any of these daily women that's got any cleaning to do, they can come to me for the key and 'and it back at the end of the day. But Mrs. Green, she got these keys direct, Potters' and Connells' —had them for days and made fuss enough about giving them up. But I would have them, and when I told her I'd mention it to the police she give in. And give me her notice too, and won't be no loss.''

"Hadn't you better come in?" said Peter. "And what do you expect me to do with all these keys? I always lose my own.''

Rush came as far as the threshold.

"And when you speak about losing keys," he said in his severest voice, "there's a matter that I'll mention. Mr. Ross, he lost one of the keys of his flat a matter of ten days ago. There's three keys to every flat, all Yales, and Mr. Ross, he lost one of his.''

"How? I do wish you'd come in, Rush.''

"I won't come no farther. In my opinion Mr. Ross left that key sticking in his door and someone pinched it. I've found it there before now myself and got sworn at for my pains.''

Peter took him by the arm, pulled him in, and shut the door.

"Look here, Rush, that might be important. Did you tell the police?''

"What's the good of them? No, I didn't tell them, but I'm telling you. And when Mr. Ross forgot himself and as good as said I'd been meddling with his papers, I said to him then, 'Mr. Ross,' I said, 'what about that key you left sticking in the door? Someone took that key, and someone took it because they was a-going to use it'—that's what I said. But now I've got something else to say. You find the one that took that key, and you'll find the one that shot Mr. Ross."

Peter made a queer sort of a face.

"A bit drastic, Rush. How do you make that out?"

"I don't have to make it out. It's as plain as the nose on your face, Mr. Peter. If I find the cat in the larder lapping up the milk, and come another day there's the fish missing, well, I don't have to make it out that it was the cat took both. You find who wanted a key to Mr. Ross's flat and why they wanted it, and you'll find out who shot him all right."

Peter looked hard at him.

"Ross made a row with you about his papers. What exactly did he say?"

There was a momentary sparkle under the bushy eyebrows.

"Better not to say exactly, in case of Miss Lucy or Miss Lee being about."

"Language?"

"Plenty. But what it come to was that someone had been turning over the papers in his despatch-box. I'd Peterson's key whilst he had a day off. Mr. Ross was out all day, and he'd left his own bunch of keys lying on the writing-table. Mortal careless he was. And next day he had me in and said I'd been at his despatch-box—said his papers had been all turned over. And I reminded him then about the key as he'd lost, but he was past listening to reason, so I just turned my back and walked out. And there was that snivelling hen of a Mrs. Green a-listening on the landing, and I'll go bail it was she as told the police I'd been given the sack. And that's what I'd like to know about, Mr. Peter. Thirty years I've been here barring the war, and I'm not taking no notice from no one, but if I'm not going to be trusted I'll be giving you my notice now, and I'll not be responsible for the keys any more."

"Good Lord, Rush!" said Peter. "What do you expect me to do with your keys, or your notice either? Why, I remember you putting me across your knee and giving me half a dozen of the best when I broke Miss Lucy's window with my catapult."

Rush relaxed grimly.

"A proper young snip, you was! And it wasn't the window altogether—you'd got me on the side of the head if I remember rightly, and if it had been my eye, where should I have been?"

Peter clapped him on the shoulder.

"Where you are now—porter at Craddock House, I expect. Get along on with you, and take your keys with you!"

CHAPTER

XXXI

WHEN HE HAD shut the door behind Rush Peter turned round, began to cross the hall, and then suddenly stood still. A couple of minutes went by before he said just under his breath, "I wonder—" And then, "well, we'll have a look-see."

Next moment he was pulling Lee up out of her chair.

"Shake off dull sloth and come along with me! I want to go through Ross's despatch-case, and it's just as well to have a witness."

"I thought the police had been through everything."

"They have, my child, and made neat lists. I don't think I'm going to find another will, or a confession that he was going to commit suicide with his left hand, or anything like that, but Rush has got a yarn about a missing key and Ross having taken it into his head that he had been routing round amongst his papers. Just imagine how he went through the roof. And now he's quite sure that the person who pinched the key and messed up the papers is the person who shot Ross. So I rather thought I would go through the despatch-case and see whether there was anything there which might— well, I don't see what it might do."

"If there was anything there, the police would have found it."

"It might be something which didn't mean anything to the police."

They went into the flat and lifted the despatch-case on to the table.

"You know," said Lee, "I can't think what you expect to find. If someone did take Ross's key and come in here to look for some paper or other, well, they'd have taken it away, wouldn't they?"

"If they found it," said Peter, trying keys.

He found the right one and threw up the lid, disclosing a tray with some odds and ends of jewellery, a gold pencil-case, an old-fashioned fob and seals, a small ivory snuff-box, and a thin bundle of letters in a rubber band. Peter took them out.

"Two notes from Mavis. I wonder how fond he was of her—there's no accounting for tastes."

"Peter, don't read them."

"I wasn't going to. But as a matter of fact anybody could. They're only answers to invitations—nothing to them at all—a couple of lines, and her name scrawled all across the page. You know, that does look as if he'd rather gone off the deep end about her. You don't keep the ordinary social note locked away like that unless you've got it pretty badly."

Lee stood by the table frowning.

"I don't like it," she said "—other people's letters. Peter, don't!"

He said very seriously, "I think I will, Lee. I've got to clear this thing up in my own mind."

The next letter was on stiff paper and typed.

"From old Prothero—

'DEAR MR. CRADDOCK,

In pursuance of our conversation on the morning of the tenth instant, I would beg to urge upon you very seriously the necessity of providing against an intestacy. The unsettled property which passed to you under your mother's will has so greatly appreciated in value on the termination of the long-term

leases granted by her grandfather, the late Mr.
Margetson Ross, that I cannot believe that you will
any longer delay to make testamentary dispositions
of what amounts to a considerable fortune.

Yours sincerely,
THOS. PROTHERO.'

"Old Prothero says Ross really was going to play. The
conversation, I gather, was all about Aggie, and good nippy
things like—did he really want her to scoop the lot if he
walked under a bus on his way home, or words to that
effect. Prothero is shaken to the core at the idea of old
Margetson Ross's unearned increment going into Aggie
Crouch's pocket. Well now, to proceed. . . . There are two or
three more letters from Prothero about the falling in of those
leases—and that's all here."

The second tray held quite a number of letters put up in
small bundles and neatly docketed—Ada; Stella; Pat; Linda;
Ninon; Marie.

Peter whistled softly.

"Bit of a lad Ross—wasn't he? I don't really think these
can have anything to do with the affair, but you never can
tell."

"There won't be anything there," said Lee wearily.
"How can there be? If someone shot Ross to get back some
letter or paper, well, they wouldn't come away without it,
would they?"

"I don't know," said Peter. "They might if they were
frightened—or disturbed. But anyhow that wasn't what I
had in my mind."

"What did you have?"

"I don't quite know," he said.

There seemed to be nothing of importance in the letters.
Ninon wrote in French, and Ada could not spell. Stella was
frankly out for a good time and as much money as she could
get. Pat had finished on a blazing row. The date was the
year before last—and a great deal of water flows under that
sort of bridge in eighteen months. Linda used the pathetic

stop, and it was noticeable that only two of her letters had been preserved. Pathos wouldn't go at all well with Ross.

Peter dropped the packets back.

"As you say, nothing there. And the rest are just business things by the look of them."

But under the business papers a final packet came to light, quite unbelievably labelled "Miss Bingham." Peter stared at it incredulously.

"Darling, am I seeing things, or does this docket say what I think it does?"

"It says, 'Miss Bingham,'" said Lee, looking over his shoulder.

"Gosh!" said Peter.

He removed the rubber band. There were three letters. He unfolded the first and read aloud:

"'DEAR MR. CRADDOCK,

I really fail to understand your letter. I am *no gossip*, but I conceive that I am entitled to my own opinion.

I remain yours truly,
WILHELMINA BINGHAM.'"

The date was June 15th of the current year.

"This," said Peter, "is highly intriguing. What had Miss Bingham been *no gossip* about?"

"Mavis and Ross, I should think," said Lee.

"We have now a second letter dated June the twentieth.

"'DEAR MR. CRADDOCK,

I am quite at a loss to understand your tone. I have never received such a letter in my life, and I shall most certainly consult my solicitor. I do not know what you mean by talking about slander. I am sure I have never said anything but the truth, and if that is an offence it is not my fault.

Yours truly,
WILHELMINA BINGHAM.'"

"She was beginning to get rattled. And here, in number three. . . . Oh Lord, I think—yes, I'm sure she must have been to her solicitor. Listen to this!

> 'DEAR MR. CRADDOCK,
>   I much regret that any remarks of mine should have been reported to you as reflecting upon your character, or on that of any other member of a family with which I have been on terms of close friendship for years. Since you desire me to say so in writing, I acknowledge that I was misinformed. I regret the words attributed to me—you do not tell me who your informant was—and I hereby tender you a sincere apology for anything I may have said. I hope that you will be satisfied with this, and that you will now relinquish any idea of taking legal proceedings.
>   Yours truly,
>   WILHELMINA BINGHAM.' "

"I wonder what she said," said Lee.

Peter laughed.

"I think one can guess. I begin to have some respect for Ross. Well, I'm afraid I don't think she would have gone the length of shooting him to get these letters back."

Lee said "No—" in a doubtful voice, then turned on him with sudden passion.

"Peter, it's horrible! We're all suspecting each other— we're ready to suspect anyone! A thing like this puts the clock back about a million years, and we're all in the jungle again with everyone's hand against everyone else. I should be glad if it were Miss Bingham, and so would you. Doesn't it show what this has done to us already? She's never done us any harm."

"Speak for yourself, darling," said Peter coolly. "Personally, I consider her a menace—Wilhelmina the Unwanted."

Lee steadied herself, gulped, and said,

"Sorry, Peter. I didn't mean to do that. What are you

going to do with the letters—tear them up or give them back to her?''

Peter grinned.

"Which do you think she'd like least? She must be wondering about them, you know. I might ring her up and say, 'Fly! All is discovered.' Or I might write a polite little note beginning, 'Dear Miss Bingham—''"

Lee grabbed his arm and pinched it severely. With her left hand she pointed at the door. It was opening slowly. Round the edge of it appeared Miss Bingham's fuzzy fringe, her marked dark eyebrows, her firm red cheeks, and her jutting upper lip. The sharp eyes darted their inquisitive glances at Lee with her hand on Peter's arm, at Peter and the open despatch-case with its tumbled papers. She showed all her teeth in an ingratiating smile and said brightly,

"The outer door was ajar, and, do you know, I thought I heard my name. I hope I don't intrude."

Lee pinched again, because she was so dreadfully afraid that Peter was going to say "You do." She said hurriedly,

"Oh, no, of course—we were just sorting some papers."

"Oh, yes—naturally. So nice of you to help, Mr. Renshaw. But don't you find it very trying—a great strain? The very room in which such a shocking crime took place. But perhaps you are not psychic. All the Binghams are intensely psychic. My grandmother, who was a Bingham of the younger branch and married her cousin—dear me, what was I saying? Oh! Why, Mr. Renshaw—are not those my letters? I—yes, *surely!*"

She had arrived at the table, and with the last word pounced on the three letters which were lying where Peter had thrown them down. He laughed a little and said,

"Did you come to fetch them?"

Her eyes darted maliciously at him. Her fingers began to fold and unfold the sheets of stiff, old-fashioned paper.

Peter said, "Is this the first time you have come for them, Miss Bingham?"

"I don't know what you mean, Mr. Renshaw."

"Sure you don't?"

"I don't know what you are talking about." She began to

tear the letters across and across, and across again, her hands moving so fast that it was done almost before they had known what she was going to do. "I am really quite at a loss"—it was the phrase she had used in one of those torn letters—"quite, quite at a loss. Mr. Craddock and I were on perfectly friendly terms until someone made mischief—and if this is a free country I cannot see why one is not entitled to one's own opinion!" Her voice trembled with anger. Her hands trembled so much that the torn fragments she was holding fell from them and strewed the floor. "And so I told my solicitor, but he wouldn't listen to me—a most disagreeable man. And he made me write what I consider an extremely humiliating letter, Mr. Renshaw, which is now, I am pleased to say, torn up. And I won't disturb you any longer, Miss Fenton. You seemed to be very busy *indeed* when I came in. I can see when I'm not wanted, I can assure you."

The sitting-room door banged, the outer door banged. Lee said,

"*Well!*"

Peter put his arm round her waist.

"I wonder whether she had been back for those letters before," he said.

CHAPTER
XXXII

Lucy Craddock leaned back in her chair with a sigh. "Oh, my dears, this does seem to have been a terribly long week."

"It's not a week yet," said Lee wearily. "This is only Saturday, and last Saturday I was in Paris with the Mervilles."

Incredible that the time in Paris with the Mervilles should in retrospect appear quite pleasant. She put this into words, and got a piercing glance from Peter.

"Perhaps you feel sorry you didn't elope with your dago friend."

"Almost, darling," said Lee, with a momentary sparkle.

"Too dreadful!" said Lucy Craddock. "I have often thought that it would be such a comfort if some sort of an interval could be arranged—when something dreadful has happened, I mean—like they do in a play. The curtain goes down, and when it goes up again it is next week, or next month, or next year. Such a good arrangement."

"Lucinda, you're a genius," said Peter. "Personally, I vote for next year, by which time Lee and I will be married and at a comforting distance of about six thousand miles from Scotland Yard. Of course, it's not quite so much as the crow flies."

Lee actually laughed.

"Do crows fly to India?"

"I don't know. Probably not. But the point, my darling child, is that policemen don't."

The telephone bell rang from the hall. Lucy Craddock began to flutter.

"Oh, my dear boy, if it is Phoebe Challoner, I really don't think I feel equal—she's so very kind, but—"

"You are still utterly prostrated," said Peter.

He departed, took up the receiver, and prepared to repel female friends in general and Miss Challoner in particular. But the voice which came to him along the wire was unmistakably male. It said in gruff, agitated accents,

"Hullo! Who's there? I want to speak to Mr. Renshaw."

"Speaking," said Peter gloomily, because the voice was beyond all question that of Bobby Foster, and to ring him up and if possible drag him into being an accessory after the fact was just the sort of thing that Bobby was likely to do.

The voice became even more agitated.

"Peter, I'm in the most awful jam—"

"And you'll be in a worse one if you start babbling on the telephone, my lad."

"You know who's speaking?"

Peter groaned.

"I do. What do you want?"

"I'm in the most awful jam. I lost my head—you know, when I got to the office it came over me. I didn't think anyone would believe me. I lost my head and bolted. I haven't got any money. That's why I rang up. If you could let me have a tenner—and meet me—"

"Dry up!" said Peter. "I want to think." He concentrated a horrible frown upon the instrument for about a minute and a half, and then spoke rapidly into the receiver.

"Are you there? Well now, listen! You know the church where the Beaver was married—well, go there, stand in the porch, and look out for me. I don't know if anyone is interested in my movements—I shall have to make sure about that. If I can get my car out I will. Look out for me and nip in the moment I stop. If I'm on foot, let me get past and then follow me. Don't speak to me until I stop and blow my nose. If you've got that, say yes, and don't say anything more. Got it? . . . All right." He hung up, opened the sitting-room door, and called Lee.

"It wasn't anyone for you, Lucinda. I've got to go out for a bit."

He took Lee into the kitchen and shut the door.

"Listen! That was Bobby. I'm going to meet him. I shall do my best to persuade him to give himself up, but if he won't, I shall have to let him have some money. How much have you got?"

"Five pounds seven and elevenpence halfpenny."

"I'll take the fiver. Better not tell Lucinda. Don't worry."

He got his car without any trouble, and after driving round the same block several times decided that Scotland Yard was not having him watched. He proceeded, therefore, to the church of St. Peter, Frith Street, and with a final glance out of his back window drew up by the kerb. Bobby Foster, embarrassingly large and conspicuous, emerged from the porch, snatched the door open, and plunged heavily in beside him. As the door slammed, the car moved off again.

Peter turned the corner with relief. Bobby was panting in his ear.

"Peter—it's been awful! You've no idea how awful it's been."

"Oh, haven't I?"

"It's a marvellous bit of luck your bringing the car. You know, I've lost my nerve. I'm afraid to go near a station in case—"

"I should think you'd be arrested at once if you did. I suppose you know there's a warrant out against you?"

The wretched Bobby dithered.

"I know—I know. I bought a paper, and it said—Peter, you can't think what it feels like to see that sort of thing—in the papers—about oneself."

Peter turned into a dull and deserted street and stopped the car.

"Now, Bobby—what's this all about anyhow? You'd better make a clean breast of it."

"Peter, I swear—I mean, I wouldn't kill anyone—you know I wouldn't. You say that sort of thing—everyone does—but you don't mean it. I mean, I loathed Ross quite a lot because of Mavis, and I won't say I wouldn't have liked to get my hands on him. But, Peter, I swear I wouldn't shoot a man just because I loathed him—Peter, I *swear* I wouldn't!''

''All right, you've said it. I've got that. Now calm down and tell me what happened after I pushed you off home on the Tuesday night.''

Bobby clutched his head.

''I don't remember an awful lot about it. Did you push me off home?''

''I did, my lad. You had been looking on the wine when it was red to a very marked extent, also on the whisky when it was yellow, and possibly on the gin when it was white.''

Bobby shook his head.

''Not gin—I loathe it.''

''Well, I should think it was the only one of the lot you hadn't been sampling, and I gather from the proceedings at the inquest that you carried on the good work after you got home.''

''I don't remember much about that either,'' said Bobby.

''Well, suppose we get on to something that you do remember.''

Bobby took out a very grimy handkerchief and mopped his brow.

''Well, I do remember saying something about shooting Ross. But I didn't mean it. Peter, you know I didn't really mean it.''

''That's all right. Carry on.''

Bobby mopped again.

''Well, the first thing that's really clear is coming up on to the landing outside Ross's flat.''

''How did you get into the house?''

''I don't know—the door must have been open.''

''Well, you were on the landing—''

''And the door of his flat was open—I could see a light—so I just walked right in. The sitting-room door was open too, and the light was on, and when I got inside, there he was, lying dead in the middle of the floor, and I got such a shock that if the door hadn't been there to take hold of, I'd have gone down too.''

"What did you do?"

"I didn't do anything—I just stood there looking at him. And the funny thing is that I was as sober as a judge. I remembered what I'd said about shooting him, and I thought, 'If anyone finds me here, I'm done.' ''

Peter took him by the arm.

"Bobby—where was the revolver? Was it in his hand?"

"Yes, it was—it was in his hand."

"Then why didn't you think it was suicide?"

Bobby stared.

"I don't know—I didn't. I thought they'd put it on me, and I legged it. The stairs were all dark, but there was a light in the hall, and the hall door was open."

"Do you know what time it was?"

"Yes, I do. That's one of the things I remember. There was a clock on the mantelpiece. It was five and twenty minutes to three."

A tingling excitement ran through Peter's veins.

"Man—are you sure about that? Don't say you are if you're not."

Bobby stared reproachfully.

"But I am sure—really. Didn't I tell you I was as sober as a judge? Seeing him lying there like that—well, it was the most awful facer. It brought me up with a jerk. I keep seeing it every time I shut my eyes."

"The point is, did you see the clock?"

"Well, I did. It's one of those square, chromium-plated ones, and it's got bright green figures on the face, and the hands were between half past two and five-and-twenty to three."

"Then," said Peter, "it wasn't you that Lucinda saw run down the steps at a quarter past two."

"Did she see someone?"

"I don't think there's the slightest doubt but that she saw Ross's murderer. Unfortunately she can't identify him. She only saw a shadow."

"At a quarter past two?"

"Yes. She found the front door open just as you did, and the door of the flat and the sitting-room door, and Ross lying dead with his own revolver in his hand and Mavis's powder compact on the floor beside him. And when she saw that, she picked the compact up and ran out of the house, leaving everything open. Now the police found your fingerprints on the banisters and the sitting-room door, and half London heard you threatening Ross on Tuesday night, so when you bolted it seemed perfectly clear to the official mind that you had shot Ross and that Lucinda had seen you getting away. The only thing that nobody has been able to explain is how you got in—and that's a card you'll have to play for all it's worth, my lad. You couldn't get in without a key unless the front door was open, but the front door was left open by the murderer at two-fifteen or thereabouts, and you found it open when you rolled up at half past two. By the way, what have you done with Mavis?"

Bobby's mouth fell open.

"Mavis?"

"Mavis," said Peter firmly. "What have you done with her?"

"I haven't done anything."

"Where is she then?"

Bobby registered surprise.

"Isn't she at home?"

"She is not. She walked out of the house on Friday morning and hasn't been seen since. She is supposed to be with you, and Lucinda is frightfully upset about it. It is apparently worse to be compromised than to be arrested for murder."

"But this is awful! Where can she be?"

"Perfectly safe, I am sure—you can trust Mavis for that. Now look here, Bobby, I've got that tenner you asked for in my pocket. If you shot Ross, take it and make the best get-away you can. But if you didn't—*if you didn't*—take my advice and come along with me to Scotland Yard."

"Give myself up?"

"You've got it in one."

"But they'll arrest me."

"Bound to. But they'll do that anyhow. If you come along of your own accord, say you got the wind up and bolted, and then tell the yarn you've just told me, you'll get a much better kick-off than if you're arrested in some purlieu after a nerve-racking time of dodging the police. They'll get you in the end, so you might as well save yourself the wear and tear and come willingly."

Bobby came.

CHAPTER
XXXIII

INSPECTOR LAMB SAT immovably in his office chair. Mr. Peter Renshaw had been talking for some time. There might be something in what he said, but then again there might not. Time would show. It was a good job getting Foster under lock and key. There was always a lot of chatter about the police if they let anyone slip through their fingers. Mr. Renshaw had done a good job there, persuading him to come in. All in his own interests too, if he was innocent.

Mr. Renshaw reached his peroration.

"It's the timetable you've got to concentrate on, Inspector—you must see that—the timetable, and that outside door. Rush shuts it at eleven. I come in at twelve, find it shut, and leave it as I find it. Ross and Miss Grey come in at one o'clock. I don't see how anyone is going to argue that they left the door open. Ross opened it with his latchkey—and he withdrew the key, because it was found on him. To my mind it's quite impossible to suppose that he did that, and didn't shut the door. Now the murderer went out of that door at a quarter past two and left it open. Miss Craddock, arriving a moment later, finds it open, finds Ross dead, and runs out of the house, leaving all the doors open behind her. About ten minutes or so later Bobby Foster rolls up. He finds the doors open. He finds Ross dead, and the shock sobers him. He says he noticed the clock on the mantelpiece particularly, and that the time was between half past two and five-and-twenty to three. Being sober, he realizes his position and legs it, leaving all doors open. Rush finds the street door open in the morning. Meanwhile Miss Fenton walks in her sleep. She is already standing over Ross with the revolver in her hand when Miss Grey comes in to get the bag she left there earlier in the evening. This was somewhere between ten and five minutes to three. Miss Fenton drops the revolver and wanders back to her own flat. Miss Grey kneels down by Ross to see if he is really dead and gets her dress stained, then looks for her bag, finds it, and comes away, switching off the sitting-room light and shutting the door of the flat. That's when Miss Bingham saw her the second time. All this is what Miss Grey told her aunt, and it is what decided Miss Craddock to volunteer her statement, because of course if Miss Craddock saw Ross dead at two-fifteen, Miss Grey's presence in the flat at three o'clock no longer exposes her to suspicion.''

The Inspector broke the pause which followed.

"First of all," he said, "Miss Craddock's statement is uncorroborated. Secondly, Mr. Foster's statement is uncorroborated. She says she was there at two-fifteen. He says he was there at two-thirty. They've both got very strong motives for mentioning those particular times, Miss Craddock because she clears her niece, and Mr. Foster because he clears himself."

"Bobby Foster didn't know about Miss Craddock's statement. He didn't know that the time he mentioned would clear him."

"It was in the papers," said the Inspector.

Peter made an impatient gesture.

"I tell you he didn't know it! Good Lord, man, you've seen him! He couldn't act to deceive a child—you must see that."

"That's as may be. Then there's another thing. You say Mr. Craddock couldn't have left the front door open when he came in with Miss Grey. But Miss Craddock found it open at a quarter past two. She says she saw someone come down the steps. Well, our theory is that this someone was

Mr. Foster. You say it couldn't have been, because Mr. Foster hadn't got a key and how did he get in? Well, who had got a key? We've communicated with the other tenants. They are all in the places where they are supposed to be, and they've all got their keys with them—I'm talking about the street door keys. Do you see where that leaves us? If Mr. Craddock didn't leave that door open himself, then someone inside the house came down and opened it—and who would be so likely to let Mr. Foster in as Miss Mavis Grey? You'll say how did she know he was there, but you've got to remember it was a hot night and all the windows were open and the curtains back. She may have seen him from her window, or he may have attracted her attention."

"He didn't know she was there, man!"

"He was afraid she might be. And he was drunk—you've got to remember that. He'd do things a sober man wouldn't. He may have called her name. There's no evidence about that. But if you're going to say, 'How did he get in?' then I'm going to say, 'why shouldn't Miss Grey have let him in?' It's no good just saying he hadn't got a key."

Peter ran his hands violently through his hair.

"The whole thing's crazy! Sober or drunk, Bobby never shot anyone. But look here, talking about keys, did Rush tell you that one of the keys of Ross's flat went missing about ten days ago? He sticks to it that someone pinched it to get at Ross's papers, and he firmly believes that this someone came back and shot Ross on Tuesday night."

The Inspector moved a slow gaze to Peter's face and kept it there.

"This is the first I've heard about that, Mr. Renshaw. What does he say?"

"Says the key went missing—thinks Ross left it sticking in the door and someone pinched it—says Ross raised Cain about his papers being disturbed, and forgot himself to the extent of accusing Rush of having disturbed them."

"Yes, we got that part. The daily woman, Mrs. Green, was listening in. She made a statement about the quarrel, and Rush admitted it afterwards—very reluctantly."

Peter leaned forward.

"Did she mention the key?"

"I don't think so." He opened a drawer. "I've got her statement here, but I'm sure there wasn't anything about a key." He turned some pages and extracted a type-written sheet. "Here we are: 'I heard it with my own ears as I was coming across the landing.' She was listening of course. An eavesdropping woman—we know her sort. Well, she goes on, 'Mr. Craddock, he was in a proper shouting rage. He says as loud as a bull, "You've been mucking up my papers!" and Rush, he answers him back as bold as brass, "And what would I want with your papers, Mr. Ross?" Mr. Craddock says, "How do I know what you want? Blackmail, I shouldn't wonder!" and Rush says, "You did ought to be ashamed of yourself, Mr. Ross." And Mr. Craddock says, "Get to hell out of here!" and Rush come out.' Well, there's nothing about a key there, you see."

Peter said, "This is what Rush said to me. He said Ross had him in and accused him of having been at his despatch-box, and he said he reminded him then about the key that he had lost, but he was past listening to reason, so Rush said he turned his back and walked out. 'And there was that snivelling hen of a Mrs. Green on the landing.' That's what he said. Now why didn't your eavesdropping Mrs. Green hear that bit about the key, or if she heard it, why didn't she pass it on? It was obviously a most important piece of evidence. Why didn't she tell you about it?"

"For the matter of that, why didn't Rush tell us?"

Peter laughed.

"Did Rush give you the impression that he would tell you anything he could possibly help? If he made a statement, I bet you had to drag it out of him word by word, whereas Mrs. Green is definitely one of the chatty kind. So why this reticence about that very important key? Do you know, I'm beginning to wonder whether she pinched it herself."

The Inspector's eyebrows rose a fraction.

"And I'm beginning to wonder whether that key was ever pinched at all. Rush says it was now, but he's taken a good long time to think that story up. He says he reminded Mr.

Craddock about the loss when they were quarrelling, but
Mrs. Green, who was listening to their quarrel, doesn't say
anything about a key. I'll have her asked the direct question,
but to my mind Rush is trying to put this key story over to
clear himself of suspicion about Mr. Craddock's papers."

Peter got up.

"Well, I think that's bunk. And bad psychology. Rush is
a crusty old cobblestone, but he's neither a thief, a blackmailer,
nor, if you're interested, a murderer. I've known him since I
was three years old, and if it comes to taking his word
against that eavesdropping wet blanket of a Mrs. Green,
well, I'd do it every time."

The bell of the telephone on the desk punctuated this
remark. The Inspector made no attempt to answer Mr.
Renshaw. He put the receiver to his car, listened for a
moment, and then said, "Put her through." A faint, shrill
sound became audible. Peter, uncertain whether to go or
stay, heard it like the thin ghost of a woman's voice a long
way off. He thought the lady was agitated, and he thought
she was in the duce of a hurry, but he caught no words. The
Inspector said, "Yes, that will be all right. I'd like you to
come along here at once if you will. . . . Yes, I was wanting
to see you. . . . No, we'll look after you—you needn't be
frightened." There was a rustling and a squeaking on the
line. The Inspector gave a deep, hearty laugh. "What—in
broad daylight? Nonsense! You come right along and don't
worry." There were more agitated sounds from the telephone. The Inspector said, "Now, now—you come right
along and we'll talk about it." He hung up and looked
across at Peter.

"That," he said, "was Mrs. Green, and she's scared to
death."

"What's she got to be scared about?"

"She says she's got something on her mind—something
she held back and didn't tell because she was afraid to. She
was talking from a call-box at Charing Cross, and you heard
me tell her to come right along."

Peter thought, "And what am I expected to say to that?
You're looking at me very hard, my good Lamb. I wonder

what that dreep of a woman was bleating into your ear just now. And which would look more like a guilty conscience, a request to stay and meet the lady, or a simple manly disposition to mind my own business and leave you to get on with your job?'' He decided on the latter course, was aware of the inspectorial eye upon him even to the door, and walked down a long corridor with the feeling that it was still boring into his spine.

CHAPTER
XXXIV

PETER WALKED BACK to Craddock house. It took him an hour because he sat for a while in St. James's Park and thought intensively about a number of things which had been disturbing his mind for the last hour or two. One of these things was so preposterous that it gave him a sensation of giddiness whenever he contemplated it. He therefore got up, walked on, and tried to think about getting married to Lee and taking her six thousand miles away from Scotland Yard. It was a paradisiacal prospect, but he failed to invest it with even a semblance of reality. And once more, up from the troubled waters of his mind, there bobbed the perfectly preposterous idea—fantastic and elusive as the sea-serpent and as tenacious of its mythical existence.

He got home and was met by Lee on the landing.

"Peter, I thought you were never coming. The Pet Lamb has been ringing up from Scotland Yard—twice."

Peter felt cold about the feet. He said, "What did he want?" and Lee pulled him into the hall and shut the door. Even then she spoke in a whisper.

"He wanted to know whether Rush was at home—*Rush*, Peter. And when I said no, he always had Saturday afternoon and evening off—you know he goes to see Ellen and her husband, and a sort of cousin person comes in to sit with Mrs. Rush—the Lamb asked when he would be in, and I said half past ten, because he always puts Mrs. Rush to bed then. And then he wanted to know whether you had got back.''

''When was this?''

''About twenty minutes ago. And he said please would I go down and get him Ellen's address from Mrs. Rush, so I did. And about five minutes ago he rang up again and wanted to know whether you had come in—and don't you think you'd better ring him up?''

''No, I'm hanged if I do!'' said Peter. He laughed angrily. ''Let's hope that's not an omen. If you ask me, I think we're going stark, staring mad, and that old Lamb will probably finish up by arresting us all.''

''What does he want?'' said Lee in a frightened voice.

''I can't imagine—I was with him an hour ago. But I know what I want, and that's a long, cold drink. Also I want to talk to Lucinda—presently, when I feel strong enough. Oh, I suppose I had better get old Lamb over first.''

Lee stood waiting whilst he rang up and was put through. She waited for Peter to speak, but after he had given his name and said, ''I hear you rang me up,'' all the talk seemed to be coming from the other end of the line. She saw Peter's eyebrows go up, and at last she heard him say, ''Yes, I suppose it took me about an hour. I sat in the Park for a bit.'' There was another interval. Then Peter said pleasantly, ''One isn't always thinking about an alibi, you know,'' and then, after a hiatus, ''I suppose you'll arrest me on the spot if I tell you to go and boil your head. . . . Yes, I thought as much, so perhaps I won't do it after all. Am I allowed a quotation instead—from Alexander and Mose? 'Clarify yo'self, boy—clarify yo'self.' '' He jabbed the receiver back upon its hook, turned a pale, determined countenance on Lee and said,

''Lamb really has gone off the deep end. He seems to think that (a) Rush, (b) I, or (c) Rush and I, have abducted Mrs. Green.''

Lee stared back. It must be a joke, but she began to feel

frightened. She said, "Why?" and Peter came and put an arm round her waist.

"An elopement with Mrs. Green sounds grim, doesn't it?"

"Is it a joke? I—I don't like it very much."

"No, it's not a joke. He's quite serious. You see, when I was with him just now Mrs. Green rang up from a call-box at Charing Cross. She said she'd got something to tell— about Ross's murder—and old Lamb told her to come right along and spill the beans. I'm piecing it together from what I heard and what he told me. He kept saying that they would look after her and she needn't be frightened, and then she said another piece, and he told her again to come right along. And then he rang off, and looked at me very hard and said, 'That was Mrs. Green, and she's scared to death.' And he told me she'd got something on her mind—something she hadn't told before because she was afraid."

"Yes—" said Lee rather faintly, because the frightened feeling was getting worse.

"Well, now he says Mrs. Green never turned up. She was speaking from Charing Cross over an hour ago, and she never turned up. It couldn't possibly have taken her more than ten minutes to get to Scotland Yard, *but she never turned up*. After about half an hour or so he sent a minion down to where she lives. The minion has just rung up, and there's no sign of her either at the house where she lodges or at the local pub which, I gather, sees a good deal of her in her off time. Lamb says she was all set to come and see him, and if she didn't come, why didn't she? And he's got an answer all ready, because she told him she was afraid of being done in. And by whom? Answer quite pat again, because she told him that too. By Rush, and by me. So if Mrs. Green has by any chance come to a sticky end, Lamb will probably do his best to hang us both."

Lee pushed him away.

"I wish you wouldn't say things like that!"

"Well, Rush may have an alibi, but I haven't. I went and mooned in the Park, and there I hatched a perfectly monstrous idea, and I want to talk to Lucinda about it, so come along.''

Lucy Craddock looked up as they came in.

''Do you know, I think I was almost asleep. Not quite, you know, but very, very nearly.''

Peter brought a footstool and sat down upon it with his arms around his knees and his head tilted a little so that he could look at her. Lee went over to the window and stood there staring out. People passing, the glint of the low sun upon the bit of the river which you could just see between the trees, the smoky blue of the sky, and a piled cloud or two that looked like thunder. It was turning very hot again, but her hands and feet were cold, and something inside her was very much afraid. There was no end to the dreadfulness, no end at all. Peter said,

''Lucinda, do you think you could come over all reminiscent and chatty?''

Lucy Craddock fluttered.

''My dear boy—of course—if there is anything you want to know—''

Peter hugged his knees.

''There is. I want to have a nice heart-to-heart gossip about Aggie Crouch—Rosalie La Fay—Ross's wife. I want you to spread yourself.''

''But, my dear, I know so little. Mary and I were naturally *most* interested, but poor John was so much upset that he only told us the barest facts, and his wife refused to talk about it at all.''

''Now, Lucinda, don't tell me that you and Mary just sat down under that. After all the lady was a public character. Do you mean to tell me that you didn't go out into the highways and byways and—well, glean?''

Lucy Craddock bridled.

''Oh, my dear boy, that sounds as if we were two inquisitive old maids!''

''Why shouldn't one be inquisitive? I am, desperately, about Aggie—Rosalie—Craddock. What did you find out?''

''Very little,'' said Lucy in a regretful voice. ''Mary thought if we went to the theatrical agencies—but we didn't know their names of course, so we—we—well, my dear boy, we employed someone."

Peter's eyes danced for a moment.

"A detective? Oh, Lucinda!"

Lucy blushed.

"Oh, no, indeed—a private inquiry agent—*discretion guaranteed*—really quite a gentlemanly man. And all he found out was that she had a sister married to a corn-chandler in Hoxton, and that there was nothing against either of their characters—which of course was very disappointing."

Peter roared with laughter.

"Lucinda, you're a jewel!"

"Oh but—my dear boy—I didn't mean that at all. I mean—well, of course one wouldn't have wanted her to have done anything dreadful, but of course after all that trouble and expense—well, you know what I mean."

"Perfectly," said Peter. "And was that all?"

"Except the photographs," said Lucy Craddock in an abstracted voice. "Now I wonder whether dear Mary kept the photographs."

"I should think," said Peter out of a bitter experience, "that Mary always kept everything."

"They were in a yellow cardboard box, tied up with the ribbon from a most beautiful box of chocolates which John gave us for Christmas that year. I remember Mary wouldn't put them in the chocolate box because she said it was too good for pictures of Aggie Crouch, so she used it for her handkerchiefs."

Peter's pulses jumped.

Gosh! Suppose he had burned those photographs. He hadn't, but just suppose he had.

A drop of cold perspiration ran down his spine. He said in a difficult, halting voice,

"The bulging yellow box—in the bottom of the wardrobe?"

Lucy nodded.

"Yes, that's where they'll be, if she kept them—and she always kept everything."

Peter got up, looked at Lee's back, looked at the door,

and without a word rushed out of the room and out of the flat.

Lucy stared after him in mild surprise, but Lee never turned round. She hardly knew he had gone, so far had she withdrawn from what was going on in the room.

And then Peter came back. He had the box in his hands—an aged, battered affair with one side gaping. And he was thinking that very likely this old battered box held two people's lives—Bobby Foster's life and—better not think about the other—better just keep on thinking about Bobby. He came across the room with an odd eager look on his face, plumped down on his stool again, and set the cardboard box across Lucy Craddock's knees.

Lee turned round from the window and came slowly over to them. She knelt down by Lucy's chair and sat back upon her heels. The feeling that something was going to happen was so strong that for the moment she had neither words, nor breath to say them with.

"Yes, that is it. I felt sure that Mary would have kept it—she always kept everything."

Peter said, "Yes, she did," in rather too heart-felt a tone. Then he untied the ribbon and pulled the lid off the box. A mass of small photographs cascaded into Lucy's lap. She contemplated them in a slightly bewildered manner and said,

"Oh dear me—all the other photographs seem to be in here too. I wonder when Mary did that."

She picked up a faded *carte-de-visite* which showed a little, round-faced girl with straight hair taken back under a comb, a skirt with a lot of frills, and a tiny apron with two pockets.

"Dear Mary at the age of six," she said in a tenderly reminiscent voice.

Lee got her breath.

"Oh! It's exactly like Alice in Wonderland—even the striped stockings!"

Lucy Craddock nodded.

"I think they are very pretty. And this is our father and mother taken on their wedding trip. I never remember him without a beard, and of course that makes a man look so much older, but here you see he has only those little mutton-chop whiskers, and I always think they were so very becoming. And this is my great aunt Sabina. Goodness— how frightened we were of her! You can see she looks very severe. She was so stout that she hardly ever got out of her chair, but she kept a strong ebony stick with an ivory knob beside her, and we used to be dreadfully afraid if we made a noise or did something she didn't like that one day she would come after us, all huge and angry with the black stick tapping.''

''Definitely a menace,'' said Peter. ''Now, Lucinda, fascinating as these reminiscences are, we haven't time for them just now. Let us have the life histories of our relations when we are not all expecting to be arrested. The only relation I feel I can give my mind to at the moment is Aggie Crouch.''

''Oh, my dear boy—not a relation!'' protested Lucy Craddock in a horrified voice.

Peter looked at her reprovingly.

''My first cousin by marriage, Lucinda. Yours and Lee's a little farther off, but still definitely connected. Anyhow, I want you to concentrate on her and her photographs. Have we got to sort through all this lot to find them, or are they by themselves?''

Lucy Craddock looked quite shocked.

''Oh, by themselves—dear Mary would never have mixed them up with our relations. I think at the very bottom of the box, in one of those thin light-coloured envelopes.''

Peter turned the whole box over. A full-sized cabinet photograph of great-uncle Henry Albert Craddock slid unnoticed to the floor, aunts and cousins overflowed into the seat of the chair. The light, thin envelope wavered upon the top of the pile. Peter picked it up and read an endorsement in faded ink:

''Photographs of Ross's wife under her stage name of Rosalie La Fay.''

There were three photographs inside. Peter put in his hand and took one of them out. It was rather like taking a lucky dip, but there was nothing lucky about the draw, which was a hard, highly glazed photograph of a plump young woman in tights, with an enormous feathered hat upon her head. There was a fuzz of hair under the hat, a pair of rolling eyes very much made up, and a smile which displayed a great many not very even teeth. His heart sank like lead. The monstrous idea which he had entertained flew out of the window as he handed the picture to Lee with a casual,

"Well, I don't think much of Ross's taste."

"She was supposed to be a very clever actress," said Lucy Craddock in a doubtful voice—"very versatile. She was in a repertory company somewhere up in the north, I believe, but when she came to London she couldn't get any work there. I haven't seen the photographs for years, but I think there's one of her as an old woman. The one Lee has got was when she was principal boy in Puss and Boots."

Peter fished again, and got a severe-looking person with every hair strained back from her face and a heavy pair of spectacles on her nose. The figure had an angular look. The tight lips were primmed.

Miss Lucy nodded at the picture.

"You would never think it was the same person, would you? But it is. It was some play in which she took the part of a schoolmistress. She really was very versatile. See how different she can make herself look."

Peter took out the third photograph. As he put his hand into the envelope, Lee turned her eyes upon his face. An agonizing suspense took hold of her. It seemed to slow everything down—the beating of her heart, the movement of Peter's hand, her power to think.

She saw Peter's hand come out of the envelope with the third photograph. She saw him look at it. She saw his face stiffen and then suddenly, violently change. She found voice enough for his name, but he drowned it.

"It's true!" he said. "After all—after all—it *is* true!"

Lee said, "What?"

He got to his feet, came round behind Lucy Craddock's chair, and leaning over her held the photograph where all three of them could see it. It showed a scraggy-looking female in a battered hat, a down-at-heels dress, and a torn apron. There was a straggle of grey hair beneath the hat. A draggled crochet shawl was clutched about the neck with one hand, the other held a dustpan and brush.

Lucy Craddock said in rather a dazed voice,

"She took the part of a charwoman in some play whose name I have forgotten." Then she gave a little gasp and said, "Oh, my dear boy!"

Lee kneeled up straight. Her feet and ankles had gone to sleep. She couldn't feel them at all, but she couldn't feel the rest of her body either. Only her hand shook and shook as she put it up to find Peter. Her voice was quite steady and clear as she said,

"It's Mrs. Green."

CHAPTER

XXXV

THERE WAS A dead silence. They all looked at the picture.

Peter was the first to speak. He said, "Well, it lets Bobby out," and with that he went through to the hall and took the telephone down from its hook.

Lee got painfully to her feet. They were quite numb. Her mind felt like that too. If Mrs. Green was Ross's wife, Aggie Crouch, then what was she doing here pretending to be Mrs. Green? And where was she now?

She heard Peter at the telephone, and then she heard the click as he put the receiver back. He came in and picked up the photograph. It had fallen into Lucy Craddock's lap, where it lay in that proximity to the Craddock relations which the refinement of Miss Mary Craddock's taste had proscribed. A portion of Aunt Sabina's crinoline obscured the dustpan and brush. The head with its battered hat had come to rest on the proud shoulder of Uncle Henry Albert. He said,

"Lamb is coming round. Well, I suppose this lets us all out. Amazing—isn't it?"

Lee said, "It doesn't prove she did it."

"It will make the police sit up and think a bit. And she's rather given herself away by disappearing. Just a little bit too clever, that business of ringing up Scotland Yard saying she'd got some hush-hush evidence, and then working off the piece about being frightened of me, and of poor old Rush. The damnable thing is that it might have come off. Lee, do you realize how very easily it might have come off? By gum, she's a clever woman! What was it Lucinda said—very versatile? I'll say she is. She probably came down here in the first instance to spy out the land. Ross wouldn't give her any more money, and she may have wanted a line on him for blackmail, or even for a divorce. I wonder if she bribed old Mother What's-her-name to retire and let her in here as charwoman. Ross hadn't seen her for twenty years by all accounts. Mrs. Green was an ironclad disguise, and she put on the port-wine mark just to make quite sure. I don't suppose Ross ever really got a look at her. She had nothing to do with his flat, and it would be easy enough to keep out of his way. Even if he passed her on the stairs, she'd only got to go down on her knees and start dusting between the banisters or something like that. I shouldn't think he ever saw her face, but he might have seen it a dozen times without recognizing her. He probably remembered her like this." He reached over for the first photograph and gave a short laugh. "Tights, curves, eyes, teeth, hair—not much there that you would connect with Mrs. Green, is there? Well, there she was. And all the time someone was moving around from one lot of cheap lodgings to another, calling herself Rosalie La Fay, forwarding Aggie's letters to old Prothero, and getting his answers back. I wonder who it was. Didn't you say there was a sister?"

"Yes," said Lucy Craddock in a flustered voice—"oh, yes, a sister—but I don't remember her name."

Peter nodded.

"Probably the sister then. Anyhow somebody she could trust to hold her tongue and do what she was told. Then Aggie gets her opportunity. She finds Ross's key sticking in the door of his flat. She pinches it, and when Ross and Peterson are both out of the way for the day she goes in and has a good worry around. It was easy enough to dodge old Rush, because he's got his settled times for everything, and she'd know what they were by then. Well, we know that Ross left his own bunch of keys lying about that day. That's what he had the row with Rush about. He saw his papers had been meddled with and he accused Rush—'Clean forgot himself Mr. Ross did,' as the old boy put it to me. But it was Aggie. It must have been Aggie. And the first thing she saw when she opened that despatch-case was old Prothero's letter urging Ross to make a will, and saying that the unsettled property amounted to a very considerable fortune and he ought to provide against any possibility of an intestacy. Mrs. Green mightn't have made much of that letter, but you can bet your life that Aggie sucked it dry. If she was in any doubt she had only got to get the sister in Birmingham to go and ask the nearest solicitor. She could have copied the letter without names, or with different names, and have asked what the position of a widow would be if the husband died leaving a lot of unsettled property and no will. And I expect it was right there that she began to think of being Ross's widow in desperate earnest. I don't know how she brought it off all the same. She went home, and she went to bed drunk at half past nine. But I suppose she probably wasn't really drunk at all, and allowing for that—''

Lee caught him suddenly by the arm.

''The Connells' flat!'' she said in a breathless voice.

All this time Lucy Craddock's eyes had been round and fixed. They did not leave Peter's face, but they did not really appear to be seeing him or anything else. She blinked rapidly now, and said in a small, obstinate voice,

''Oh, no, my dear, the Connells were away. And in any case—''

''Not the Connells,'' said Lee—''*their flat*. Mrs. Green—she had their key. She said so when she was going off on the Tuesday night. She said she had just finished cleaning up after them, and Rush was furious because she didn't give him the key before she went. You know she had one of her bad turns, but I suppose it was just acting really. I am sure she just went home and pretended to be drunk so that the other people in the house would leave her alone, but I think

she slipped back here—Rush doesn't lock up till eleven—
and hid in the Connells' flat. It—it's just underneath Ross's,
and she would be able to listen and make sure that everything was quiet before she came out."

"You think she shot Ross?" said Lucy Craddock in
horrified accents.

"What do you think, Lucinda?" said Peter drily.

CHAPTER
XXXVI

W HAT INSPECTOR LAMB thought was that it wasn't going to be at all an easy job and he'd better get busy with a timetable.

"The bother is, we don't know where she may be making for. Just get on to Mr. Prothero at his private house, Mr. Renshaw, and ask whether he hasn't had any word about a change of address from the woman in Birmingham. Mrs. Green won't go to the place where her confederate has been staying, so I'll lay they've got a move planned, and when it's over it'll be Mrs. Green who has taken on being Miss La Fay, and the other will have gone back to her own name or else gone off the map altogether."

He immersed himself in the timetable. Presently Peter came back, and he looked up alertly.

"Well, what did you get, Mr. Renshaw?"

"He's on his dignity. Doesn't keep clients' addresses at his private house. Doesn't expect to be rung up on a Saturday evening. But I did drag one thing out of him. All this chopping and changing of addresses falls into the last three months, and before that Mrs. Ross Craddock was living at Doncaster under the name of Miss La Fay. You see, I thought she might go back to wherever she was living before she started being Mrs. Green."

"Did he give you the Doncaster address?"

"No, he didn't. I haven't rung off. Would you like to deal with him?"

The Inspector heaved himself out of his chair. He could be heard coping with Mr. Prothero in a highly official voice, after which he returned and addressed himself to the timetable again.

"He'll get the address and let the Doncaster police have it. Now about these trains? Let's see what she could catch—" He flicked pages, made notes, used the telephone, and turned a considering eye upon Peter. "The trouble is she isn't going to look like Mrs. Green by the time she gets anywhere at all. If she goes to this Doncaster address she goes there as Miss La Fay, and of course we can question her. But it's not going to be so easy to prove that she ever was Mrs. Green unless she's got the clothes with her. She mayn't have been able to get rid of them, or she mayn't have thought it necessary. If it hadn't been for the photographs, no one would ever have connected her with Mrs. Green. She could have gone ahead and claimed all that money, and no one would ever have dreamed of suspecting her. Mind you, we're very far from having a case against her as things stand. The best hope is that she'll give herself away. Now, Mr. Renshaw, I'm going to Doncaster, and if you like you can come along too. I'm sending Abbott to Birmingham. I make it this way. I don't suppose for a moment that the woman was really ringing up from Charing Cross—much more likely King's Cross. And she'd get the first train she could. Well, the first train's a slow one, and she had twenty minutes to catch it. She may have got out of Mrs. Green's clothes and taken the mark off her face before she rang me up, or she may have still had it to do. I should think she would have done it already, because she wouldn't want to attract attention by being seen at King's Cross looking like Mrs. Green, and twenty minutes wouldn't give her too much time for what she would have to do. She wouldn't want to hang about the station waiting for a fast train either—she'd want to get clear away out of London, because she knew she'd started a hue and cry. Now this is where we come in. There's an express thirty-five minutes from now, and it reaches Doncaster ten minutes before that slow train. If she didn't take that, she'll be taking this. So either we get to Doncaster ten minutes before she does, or we all get there together, and I'll be very glad of your assistance to identify the lady.'' He paused, turned a hard, solemn gaze upon Peter, and added, ''Always supposing she's going to Doncaster, which I don't feel at all sure about myself.''

''I'm with you,'' said Peter. ''Lucinda, lend me a pound. One needs a margin on a wild goose chase. Better make it two, or even three. She may have gone to Jericho. What happens then, Inspector? Do we charter an aeroplane? What—a whole fiver? Lucinda—how prodigal! By the way, you'd better make Lee go to bed—she's all in.'' He kissed them both and ran to catch up the Inspector, who had already begun to descend the stairs.

The last of the summer daylight was gone long before their train reached Doncaster. The Inspector displayed a most unexpected agility. As the train slowed down, he had the carriage door open and was out upon the platform before it came to rest. He and Peter stood unobtrusively on either side of the exit. A local constable came up, spoke low, and went through into the booking-hall.

Some twenty passengers had alighted. The first one or two approached the ticket-collector. A stout man in a bowler hat, with a stout wife in artificial silk and two stout little boys with apple cheeks, one flapping a banana skin and the other eating peppermints out of a paper bag. Here at least there could be no suspicion.

There followed a jaunty, shabby young man with bow legs and a loud cloth cap. He hooked a ticket out of his waistcoat pocket, thrust it at the collector with a cheerful ''Evening, George,'' and swaggered off, whistling as he went.

After him a woman with a shopping-bag full of brown paper parcels. She had a bent, discouraged look. Her hat had drifted to one side of her head. Her hair was in wisps. Her washed-out cotton dress sagged unevenly at the hem. She might have been Mrs. Green some dozen or so years ago. Peter looked at her with a sort of horror in his mind, because if this was the woman they were hunting, she seemed a most wretched and helpless prey. She sighed with utter weariness as she set down her bag and began a slow, ineffectual search for the ticket which she appeared to have mislaid. She had two pockets, a shabby handbag, and a purse. The ticket was in the purse, which was the last place in which she thought of looking for it. By the time she had given it up there was a little crowd of people waiting behind her, and Peter was quite sure that she was not Mrs. Green. Her eyes were the wrong colour. The light shone right down upon her as she looked up at the collector. It showed them hazel with faint brownish flecks. He remembered that Mrs. Green's eyes were of a washed-out bluey grey. You can't change the colour of your eyes. He looked across at the Inspector with a slight shake of the head, and, sighing heavily, the weary creature passed between them and went her way.

There was no one else who could possibly have been Mrs. Green.

The slow train came in ten minutes later, and they took up their places again, standing one on either side of the ticket-collector, but beyond him so that they were not seen by the passengers as they approached.

Only some half dozen people got out when the train stopped, and four of these were men. Of the two women one was both tall and bulky, with great cushioned shoulders, enormous hips, and a heavy rolling walk. Her large red face shone with perspiration. Her strong black hair curled vigorously under a flat fly-away hat profusely trimmed with poppies, cornflowers, and white marguerite daisies. Her expression was one of complete satisfaction with herself and with the world in general.

Last of the six came a woman in a neat dark coat and skirt and a close black hat. Copper curls rolling up from under the brim, an eye-veil standing out stiffly like an inverted halo, tinted cheeks, and a bright scarlet mouth—those things held Peter's eye. A picture of Mrs. Green, wispy, bedraggled and down at heel, rose to the surface of his mind. The woman who was coming towards them along the platform wore thin silk stockings, and shoes with flashy buckles and heels like stilts. He saw Mrs. Green's foot in a bulging shoe with a burst seam. He looked at the woman in black, and still saw Mrs. Green. It was like an effect in a film—one picture superimposed upon another, both pictures there together, flickering, combining, separating again. He felt horror, and the keenest excitement he had ever known. For no reason that he could have named he was quite sure that this was, not Mrs. Green who had served her turn and was no more, but Aggie Crouch—Rosalie La Fay—Ross Craddock's wife. No, Ross Craddock's widow—she had most efficiently seen to that.

He looked across at Inspector Lamb. His eyes gave a scarcely perceptible signal as the woman came up ticket in hand. The two of them stepped forward together and blocked her way.

The shock was absolute. It caught her on the peak of her success and knocked her spinning. The risks had all been run, the price had all been paid. She was secure, triumphant, utterly unprepared. And then, right in her path, the Inspector whom she had tricked, and Peter Renshaw whom she had left to bear the blame. She stopped, and froze before their eyes. Her chin dropped. The colour stood out ghastly on cheeks turned suddenly grey.

The Inspector's hand came down on her shoulder. He began to say his piece. "Agnes Craddock, alias La Fay, alias Green, I arrest you—" But he got no farther than that. She wrenched from under his hand, whirled round, and darted back across the platform through the first open carriage door and, banging it behind her, out on the other side.

Peter stood where he was. He had identified her, but he would do no more. He saw the Inspector snatch at the carriage door and climb in. The air was suddenly full of loud commotion and noise—the shriek of a whistle, the roar of an oncoming train. Porters ran, the ticket-collector joined them, passengers who had just given up their tickets came streaming back. He saw them run, he heard them shout, and he heard the grinding and clanging of the train which came to rest against the far platform.

The ticket-collector came hurrying back, a fair-haired man with a face like a damp dish-cloth.

"It got her!" he said, and leaned against the wall. "Ran right in front of it she did, and it caught her and knocked her flying. I dunno if she's dead or not, but I'm to ring up for the ambulance." He wiped his face with his sleeve and stumbled through into the ticket office.

CHAPTER
XXXVII

PETER RENSHAW CAME back to Craddock House on the Sunday afternoon. He thought, "Well, it's all over now. Bobby's safe, and I don't give a damn whether Mavis is safe or not. No need to either, Mavis being very well able to look out for Mavis Grey." He thought, "Lee and I can get married. I can take her right away out of this, and I hope to heaven we never see Craddock House again."

He rang the bell of Lucy Craddock's flat, and when Lee opened the door he picked her up and held her close, and didn't say a word.

When they were in the sitting-room he said in an odd, unsteady voice, "Where's Lucinda?" and Lee said,

"She's lying down. I think she's asleep."

They stood looking at each other. Lee's lips trembled. She said, "Why don't you tell me what has happened?" And Peter said,

"It's all over—she's dead. It's a good thing—better than being hanged. When she saw old Lamb and me she lost her nerve and bolted—right under a train. Horrid business. They got her to a hospital, and she was able to make a statement. Old Lamb says she was as clear as a bell. She dictated a confession. I've got a copy of it here. Come and sit down."

He took out a number of folded type-written sheets and gave them to her. She sat down on the sofa. Peter sat beside her. They read the confession together.

"My name is Agnes Sophia Crouch. My stage name is Rosalie La Fay. I married Ross Craddock at the Marylebone register office on August 25th 1917 when he was over from France on ten days' leave. That was the only time we lived together. When he came home after the Armistice he'd had enough of me. He said so. Said he'd been a fool to marry me. Said I was older than him. And if I was, I was his wife just the same. He couldn't get away from that, could he? I'd got my lines.

His father didn't like it, but he played up. There wasn't anything against me, and so I told the lawyer. And old Mr. Craddock made me an allowance. It was three hundred a year to start with, but when the depression came he cut it down. And then he cut it again, and when he died Ross brought it down to twenty-five, and then this last year he stopped it altogether. Well, I wasn't going to stand for that. How could I? I wasn't getting any younger, and jobs weren't getting any easier to find. Besides I wasn't going to put up with it. No one's ever scored me off without my getting my own back in the end. If he had treated me decently, I'd have let him alone, but he didn't know how to treat anyone, and I wasn't going to let him get away with it.

I thought I'd come up to London and smell round a bit, and I thought I'd manage it so that no one would know. I left my room in Doncaster, and I got my sister Annie—she's Mrs. Love, and a widow—to take a room in Birmingham and call herself Miss La Fay. There's enough likeness for a description of one of us to fit the other. But first and last, all Annie knew was that I'd got business in London and didn't want anyone to know I was there. She thought I was getting a divorce, and she sent my letters on to me care of the post office. She didn't know anything more than that.

Twenty years ago I played the part of a charwoman called Mrs. Brown. It wasn't much of a play, but I got the best notices I ever had. Well, I took a fancy to play the part again. I bleached my hair and painted a port-wine mark on my face, and I took a lot of pains over the clothes—to get them shabby enough, you know—and I called myself Mrs. Green. First thing I did was to get friendly with the old woman who did the daily work at Craddock House. She was getting past it, and her married daughter was wanting her to go and help with the children, so I got her to take me round and speak for me. Nobody bothers where a daily comes from.

What I thought was, if Ross wouldn't give me my allowance I could run him in for a divorce, and then he'd have to give me alimony. I hadn't any money to pay detectives, so I had to look about and find the evidence myself. Well, up to a fortnight ago I hadn't got any further, and I was getting right down sick of the whole thing. I'd enjoyed it at first, doing Mrs. Green, and taking everybody in, and feeling what a good job I was making of it, but that had worn off and I was just about as sick of it as I could be.

And then I found Ross's key sticking in the door of his flat, and I nipped it out and put it in my pocket. I got my opportunity a day or two after that. Peterson had the day off, and Ross went out after breakfast and said he wouldn't be back till late. Rush had Peterson's key, but he keeps his times like a piece of clockwork, so I knew just when he'd be out of the way. Well, I had a piece of luck. Ross had left his bunch of keys lying out on the writing-table, so I only had to help myself. I went through the drawers, but there wasn't anything there. All I found was the pistol he kept in one of them, and I didn't bother about that till afterwards. And then I opened the despatch-box, and there, right on the top, was a letter from the lawyer, Mr. Prothero, wanting Ross to make his will. It was all wrapped up very politely, and my name not mentioned, but what it amounted to was that he'd better hurry up and make a will if he didn't want me to come in for all that money of his mother's that wasn't tied up. I knew what it meant well enough, and I knew that the law had been altered, and that a widow got her rights now and not just the third that she used to get when her husband died without making a will. And it came over me that if Ross were to die before he made that will, I'd be a rich woman.

I went on turning out the despatch-box. The bottom of it was full of letters from other women. He had kept theirs—he hadn't kept any of mine. That's when I made up my mind to kill him. I put everything back, and I went away and thought out the best way of doing it.

I got it all planned. Being on the stage gives you an insight into that sort of thing. If I could get the scene set right, then it was just a matter of timing. I made up my mind I'd do it the next time he brought a girl home to supper, because I meant it to look as if they'd quarrelled and he'd shot himself. In some ways it went better than I'd planned, and in some ways it went worse. Anyhow it went different—but I suppose that's what always happens, no matter how carefully you plan.

The way I planned it was this. I'd been cleaning up Mr. and Mrs. Connell's flat after they had gone away on their holiday. That was the Tuesday, and I knew Ross was bringing someone back, because I heard him tell Peterson to put out champagne and two glasses. Miss Lucy Craddock was going off abroad, so it all suited well enough—one less person on the landing. But when I came past just to make sure she was gone I found Miss Lee Fenton was there. I told her I'd got one of my turns and I didn't think I'd be fit to come on the Wednesday. Then I went off and stayed about in the King's Arms till about a quarter past nine, and when I got to my room, there were half a dozen people besides the woman of the house ready and willing to swear I'd drunk myself stupid and was good for a dozen hours' sleep.

I'd a ground-floor room, and I always locked my door. I let them hear me snoring for a bit, and then I got out of the window and came along back to Craddock House. Rush doesn't lock up till eleven, and for twenty minutes before that he'll be putting his wife all ready for the night. I had only to watch for the street being clear and walk in.

Craddock House has an alleyway running between it and the next house. I watched from there. Then I just ran in and up the stairs and let myself into the Connells' flat, which was number five and right underneath Ross's. If I'd met anyone I was going to say I'd dropped my purse, but there wasn't anyone about, so I just sat down and waited.

I heard the front door round about twelve o'clock. I stood on a chair and looked through the fanlight over the door. That was Mr. Peter Renshaw coming in. It was an hour later when Ross came, and he had Mavis Grey with him. They went on up the stairs, and I opened my door and listened. I heard them go into his flat and shut the door, and right there it came over me, what was I going to do if she stayed there all night? I hadn't thought of that before somehow, and it made me mad with rage. I made up my mind that I would shoot them both and try and make it look as if Ross had done it—I thought I owed him that. You see, I'd planned to shoot him with his own pistol. I once had to practise shooting for a show I was in, and I turned out quite a good shot, so I knew I could manage it all right. I waited a bit so as to let them get on with the champagne, and then, just as I was thinking about it, I heard a crash right over my head. I ran to the door and opened it to listen, and there was Mavis Grey calling out, and Mr. Renshaw out of his room hushing her up, and Ross talking queer and thick as if he was drunk. And in the end Mavis went into Mr. Renshaw's flat and they shut the door.

Nothing could have been better for me. I made up my mind to wait till two o'clock, and as soon as I heard Mrs. Connell's dining-room clock strike I came out of the flat. I turned off the light on that landing, and when I got up on to Ross's landing I turned out that light too—that was in case I had to run for it. I had the key of Ross's flat all ready, but I didn't have to use it, because the door was ajar. He must have gone back in and left it like that, and when I looked round the sitting-room door I could see why. The light was on, and Ross was sitting right underneath it straddling across a chair with his arms along the back and his chin down on them. There was a lot of dried blood on his forehead and cheek, and his shirt was in such a mess that I thought someone had done my job for me. He didn't move his head or take any notice of my coming in, he just sat there staring. There was something to stare at too. The table with the drinks had been pushed over, and there was a smashed decanter, and bits of broken glass everywhere. There was some in Ross's hair—I saw it glitter under the light.

I had gloves on my hands. I went to the writing-table and got the pistol out of the drawer where Ross kept it. It was loaded when I was there before, but I opened it again to make sure. And all the time he never moved. He just kept on staring. I came over with the pistol in my hand, and when I was a yard away he put up his head with a jerk and said, 'Who's there?' He took hold of the back of the chair to pull himself up, and I thought, 'It's now or never.' There was something very heavy passing along the Embankment— all the windows rattled with it. I shot him like that, and he fell down on to the floor and never moved. That was the only mistake I made. I was on the left of him, and I fired too soon. I ought to have come round on his right, and then everyone would have believed he had done it himself. But I had to think about the lorry, because that was what I was counting on to cover up the sound of the shot. I put the pistol in his hand quickly and came away. I left the light burning, and the door of the flat ajar. I crept downstairs and opened the street door. I didn't make a sound. I was afraid to risk shutting the street door in case of waking Mr. Pyne, so I left it just pushed to, and ran down the steps and along the alleyway. It took me half an hour to get back to my room. I got in through the window and went to bed. I didn't see how anyone could possibly suspect me, and I don't see now how they did.

I planned to disappear as soon as it was safe. Annie was getting worried, and I didn't dare leave her alone too long. But I had to wait till after the inquest. I wrote to her to come down and meet me on the Saturday. She was to give up her room, and I sent her a letter for my old landlady at Doncaster to say I was coming back. Annie brought me down a suit-case and my own clothes and a transformation to cover my hair. I was puzzled to know what to do with Mrs. Green's things, but I made sure I was safe, so I just brought them along. I thought I could get rid of them later on. Annie went back to her home. She'd given out she was away nursing a sister who was ill. She never knew anything— I'm dying and I swear she didn't. She only thought she was helping me to get my divorce. I'm sorry about Annie, but I'm not sorry about Ross. I'd do it again tomorrow.''

CHAPTER
XXXVIII

LEE LET THE typewritten pages fall.

"It was you who began to suspect her! Oh, Peter—what put it into your head?"

"It was that business about the key. She was listening whilst Ross went for old Rush about his papers being disturbed, and she could tell the Inspector all about the row. But she didn't say a word about one of the keys of the flat having been pinched. Well, when Rush told me about his row with Ross he laid great stress on this missing key, and said he'd reminded Ross about it then. He said a thing which stuck in my mind. He said, 'Find the one that pinched that key and you'll find the one that shot Mr. Ross.' When I saw old Lamb at Scotland Yard I asked him whether he'd heard anything about this missing key, and he said he hadn't. He read me the bit out of Mrs. Green's statement, and she never mentioned it. I began to wonder why. Rush had been flinging it up at Ross, and it was such an obvious thing to take hold of—I didn't see how she could have missed it. But she never said a single word about that key. When I came to wonder why, I could only find one answer. It was because she had taken it herself."

"How horrible!" said Lee with a shudder in her voice.

"She very nearly brought it off," said Peter—"very, very nearly. And it might have been you, or me, or Bobby, or

Lucinda, or Mavis, or Rush, or even blameless Bingham who had to face the music. It seems to me they could have made out a pretty good case against any one of us. In fact, my dear, the only thing that saved us was the undoubted fact that we couldn't all have done it. But Bobby certainly did his best to get the rope round his neck. He and Mavis are a pair."

"Oh," said Lee, "Lucy has heard from Mavis."

"Lucy has *what?*"

"Heard from Mavis in a letter, quite calm, placid and comfortable."

"Where is she?"

"In Cornwall. She's quite casual about it, and she doesn't seem to have any idea that there's a warrant out for her arrest. She went out on the Friday morning—"

"As per Aunt Gladys—to get a breath of air?"

"Several breaths. And she met Joyce Lennox—you know, the girl with all that money and a Bentley—so Mavis told her what a fuss there had been about Ross, and how frightful Aunt Gladys and Uncle Ernest were, and what a bore the inquest was. And Joyce said, 'Well, why go to it? Why not hop in and come along down to Cornwall with me?'—just like that. So she did. And neither of them seem to have thought it mattered in the least."

"Well, I hope they give her six months for contempt of court or whatever it is."

Lee got up, wandered to the fireplace, looked back over her shoulder.

"I used to think—I very nearly thought—you liked her—"

"*Me?* My good girl!"

"*She* would have liked you to."

"Ross and Bobby not enough for her?"

Lee shook her head very slightly, was caught by the shoulders, and twisted round.

"Why are we talking about Mavis?" said Peter violently. "I haven't seen you for twenty-four hours, and first we talk about murders, and then we talk about Mavis. I want to talk about Me."

Lee looked up at him, and felt her colour rise.

"Only you?"

"Me first. Afterwards, if you are very good, we may devote a few moments to you. We begin with me because I shall burst if I can't get someone to listen to all the things that are positively seething in me about my wedding, my honeymoon—"

"Peter!"

"I shall get a licence. I've always liked the sound of a licence—a sort of off-the-deep-end flavour. I don't know where you get one, but old Prothero will know. I must ring him up. A licence, and a wedding ring—gold, or platinum? Take your time, because you'll have to wear it all the rest of your life. Honeymoon—I say, that's an atrocious word if you like—vulgarity incarnate! Cut it out! We'll go on a wedding journey instead, like the early Victorians. You can have a poke bonnet, and if you insist, I'll wear a stock. 'The bridegroom, Mr. Peter Renshaw, looked excessively handsome in a black satin stock. The bride—'"

"Peter, are you mad?"

Peter said, "Yes, darling," and swung her off her feet.

From the doorway Lucy Craddock viewed the scene with indulgence.

"Oh, my dear boy!" she breathed.

THE END

long time to think that story up. He says he remembers Mr.